# ENCHANTMENT AT DELPHI

# ENCHANTMENT AT DELPHI

## RICHARD PURTILL

GULLIVER BOOKS

HARCOURT BRACE JOVANOVICH

SAN DIEGO     AUSTIN     ORLANDO

Requests for permission to make copies of any part of the work should be mailed to:
Permissions, Harcourt Brace Jovanovich, Publishers, Orlando, Florida 32887.

Library of Congress Cataloging-in-Publication Data
Purtill, Richard L., 1931–
    Enchantment at Delphi.
    "Gulliver books."
    Summary: Fascinated by the temple ruins at Delphi, a young girl manages to slip into the site when it is deserted and finds herself involved in a strange adventure.
    [1. Space and time—Fiction.   2. Greece—Fiction]
I. Title.
PZ7.P9794En   1986      [Fic]      85-30556
ISBN 0-15-200447-5

Designed by Matthew Simpson
Title page illustration by Donna Diamond
Map by David Lindroth
Printed in the United States of America

First edition

A B C D E

*FOR MY FRIENDS*
*WHO SHARE MY LOVE OF GREECE*
*BUT ESPECIALLY FOR*

Bubbles

Polly

Ruth

Dimitri

Magda

Soula

and

Judy

Stadium

Cliffs—The Shining Ones

Line of Power

Theater

Temple
of Apollo

Rock

Path

Treasury of the
Athenians

Rock of Sibyl

Museum

Path

Line of Power

TO THE VILLAGE
OF DELPHI

DELPHI
TODAY

Ticket Booth

Gate

TO THE CASTALIAN SPRING →

TO ATHENA'S TEMPLE
AND THOLOS

N

# CHAPTER ONE

I got up to the Rock this morning, early and alone, but it was no use. I wonder if I will ever again see the mists rising from the Rock and pass through them to find the land changed yet unchanged. I wonder if I really want to; all that I truly fear as well as all that I truly love lies beyond those mists. Or does it? Can They reach out and touch me even here, though the Rock is clear and barren in the early-morning sun and only the faintest tingle in my scalp and the back of my neck tells me that the Path is still there, beyond my reach?

It was a morning full of small defeats that all turned into victories, until the last defeat. I thought that I had overslept for the first time in many days when I woke to the sound of one of the big tour buses going by in the street below. As I scrambled into my clothes, all the things that seem to happen only when you're in a hurry conspired to hold me up: a knotted shoelace on my hiking boot; my clean bra blown off the washline on the little balcony and caught on a bush below. I made myself calm down and tease out the knot carefully; then I took one of the sticks I'd picked up on the mountain to use as a hiking staff, leaned over as far as I dared, and triumphantly hooked the bra off the bush.

It was already too warm for a long-sleeved shirt. I draped my oversize sleeping T-shirt over the line to air, pulled on jeans and a regular daytime T-shirt, and clattered down the stairs in my hiking boots. Boots and jeans would be uncomfortably hot as the sun rose higher, but if I had no luck at the Rock, I wanted to be ready to push my way through the bushes on the hillside to continue my explorations of the Lines of Power.

When I went down for breakfast, Kyria Amalia had gone off to do her marketing, and the old woman who helped out in the kitchen clucked indulgently as I gulped my coffee. I made most of my breakfast bread into sandwiches with generous dollops of jam. The bread today was still fragrantly fresh from this morning's baking. Sometimes Kyria Amalia couldn't resist a bargain on yesterday's bread, and it couldn't compare with bread just out of the oven that morning. The bread was one of the things I'd miss when I left Greece—if I ever did leave.

Not having to make conversation with Kyria Amalia saved me precious moments, and while I hurried down the street, I could see that I wasn't as late as I had feared; the tour bus that woke me up must have been a really early one. I hesitated at the turnoff to the site; there had already been a small crowd in front of the museum, and tour buses were beginning to pass me as I almost ran down the highway outside the village. But I was afraid to alter my ritual: I went on to the spring, drank, and bathed my face and wrists. As I hurried back to the site, I was glad that I had wet my bandanna in the clear cold water; I was already hot and sweaty when I puffed up to the gate. I wiped my face on the cool bandanna, and then I flipped it into a roll and I tied it loosely around my neck for coolness.

My heart sank when I got a good look at the gate. Except on Thursdays, when the museum is closed, most of the tours go there before they come to the site. But today there was at least one busload of tourists waiting at the gate, being lectured in German by my least favorite guide as they waited for the site to open. I try not to think of all German tourists as pushy and inconsiderate, but darn it, some of them *are*. And some of the younger ones are annoyingly athletic, striding off up the trail so there's no chance of my getting to the Rock first and alone.

That group was not about to let me get through the gate before them, and my heart sank. But once through the gate they had to stand and wait while the guide got their tickets, and my heart gave a little bound as I saw that the friendliest guard was on duty at the entrance. I had my pass out of my wallet and ready in my hand, but he simply grinned and waved me past.

The sour-faced guard, who always reads my pass from cover to cover, grumbling under his breath, was trapped in the booth selling tickets. But he gave me a dirty look as I passed him. Actually he has a point: I *am* too young and too unqualified to have a free pass to museums and archaeological sites from the Ministry of Culture. Dear Professor Pennyquick had gallantly exaggerated my qualifications in his letter of recommendation, and I think the pretty young secretary in the museum office in Athens had stretched a point when she carried my letter and photograph into the office where they issue the passes. The grizzled Belgian scholar who was sitting nearby on the bench in the waiting room was still waiting when the secretary came out and gave me the pass. He looked at me quizzically, and the secretary smiled at me with a touch of feminine conspiracy. Greek women aren't very liberated, and some of them resent foreign women who are; but others seem to take a vicarious pleasure in helping a foreign girl do things they'd find hard to do themselves.

My heart pounded as I strode up the path past the marketplace and the treasuries, as much from anticipation as from the pace I was setting myself. I looked around apprehensively in case there were workmen on the site. Somehow I'm sure that nothing will happen at the Rock unless I'm completely alone and unobserved. At last I stood before the Rock, and so far as I could see no one was around. I looked up to the great cliffs called the Shining Ones, seeing again how from this spot the dip at the top of the cliffs made an almost perfect semicircle. Untold years ago, before earthquakes and erosion, it had been even more nearly perfect, as I had good reason to know.

I turned then and looked at the hills across the great valley. Just in line with the dip in the cliff, two hills came together to make another semicircular dip. The horns, the horns of consecration, I thought. And between them the Line of Power. I could feel a tingle of that power in my body. But it was faint, too faint. Even before I climbed up into the cleft of the Rock and found it still stark and clear with no sign of the mists, I knew that I had failed.

For a few minutes I stood there with my hands on the Rock at each side of me, my head bowed. The disappointment made me sick, and yet, underneath it all, wasn't there relief? Some things now I need not face; some decisions I need not make, might never have to make. Never? That was chillingly final, and yet there was a sort of peace in the finality. But surely it couldn't end like this, with nothing settled. I straightened up and climbed out of the cleft on the uphill side. At least there were things I could learn, could try to understand.

There were still no tourists or workmen in sight, so I took some shortcuts up around the side of the Temple and diagonally up the slope. I stopped for a moment at the little hidden cistern where water that trickles down the hill from springs above is collected and piped down the hill. I gently parted the tendrils of moss that slowly waved in the flowing water and drank deep. Then I continued up to the next rocks in the Line.

I was already far enough from the main paths to be away from the tourists. I climbed a rough gray rock and sat cross-legged on its top, looking down over the site. The tremendous silence of the mountain was hardly touched by the occasional sounds that reached me from below: a guard's whistle as a tourist strayed into forbidden territory; a tour bus gunning its engine. There were sweet smells in my nostrils from the flowers that grew in the crannies of the rock and the herbs I had not been able to avoid crushing as I climbed the rock. Below me the first tourists were coming up into the Temple—not a tour group yet, but the few adventurous ones who forged ahead to have the site to themselves for a little while.

Screened as I was by the bushes that grew in front of the rocks, they could hardly have seen me unless they knew just where to look, but I slid off my rock and began climbing farther up the hill. Over the past days I had developed rituals and habits that were irrational and superstitious—or were they? Such strange things had happened to me that I could no longer be sure what was reason and what was superstition. Perhaps it really was true that I had a better chance of making contact again if no one on the site saw me after I was clear of the gate.

I had to get my strange adventures straightened out in my own mind before I could solve any of my problems. I made up my mind to write down everything that had happened to me, to come to the site every morning and spend the rest of the day writing. Everything was still so vivid in my mind that it shouldn't take me long to write it all down, and when I had it done, I could read it over and perhaps find some pattern that escaped me now. Somehow I felt that I should start with what happened today, and I have; but now I must begin at the beginning.

It had all begun on my second day in Delphi. The first day was taken up with the bus trip from Athens, with finding my room at Kyria Amalia's little family hotel, and with exploring the village. The site was closed by the time I had unpacked my things, so I set off to check out the cheaper restaurants and find a grocery store to replenish my stock of food for lunch.

All the restaurants I found the first day seemed expensive compared to my favorite haunts in the Plaka district of Athens, and the grocery stores were closed for siesta. Luckily I had filled up on souvlakia and bread at our lunch stop in Livadia and still had bread, cheese, olives, and some oranges left in my lunch bag. So I pulled the single chair in my room out onto the little balcony and had a picnic supper while I looked down at villagers and tourists strolling along the street below. I was paying more than I had planned for this room, but I hadn't been able to resist that balcony, which made the tiny room seem a good deal larger and airier. And Kyria Amalia Nomikou, who seemed to be the owner or manager of this little rooming house which called itself a hotel, was kind and friendly, though a little inclined to be maternalistic. *Kyria* means "Mrs.," but there didn't seem to be any Kyrios (which means "Mr.") Nomikos around.

"You are student, then," she had said in her intelligible, if somewhat eccentric, English, much better anyway than my Greek. "I can see you are clever girl. You go to Mouseion, to Temple, and learn, come home read your books. These good-for-nothing boys ask you to go disco, tell them no. They don't mean good." I laughed and told her that discos didn't appeal to me. Seeing her puzzled look, I translated that as best I could, *"Then m'aressee toh deesko."* She was loud in her praises at how well I spoke Greek but kept on chattering to me in her fractured English. She let me go reluctantly when I said I had *mathemata*, which, though it sounds like "mathematics," just means "lessons" or "homework." Like most Greeks, she took learning seriously, and I found later that I could usually get away from her by pleading "lessons."

In the cool of the evening I walked out the road past the museum and site entrance and down the hill to the unfenced ruins that surround the Tholos, the few columns that remain from a circular temple which once stood there. Every picture I've seen of the temple as it was originally makes it look heavy and clumsy, but these three columns with the fragment of curved pediment atop them have an airy grace that makes them one of the loveliest works of human hands at Delphi. The columns, which have been shattered and fitted together again like a giant jigsaw puzzle, are dappled brown and white because some fragments were discolored as they lay on or in the ground and others stayed white. Generally I don't like ruins and cherish the few perfect things which have come down to us from the ancient days, like the bronze Poseidon in the National Museum. But the Tholos, I think, must be more beautiful as a ruin than it ever was when whole, and the jigsaw pattern of brown and white on the columns is a silent witness to their violent history and the loving care of the archaeologists who restored them.

As I came back through town to my room, I had several invitations to the "deesko" just as Kyria Amalia had predicted. The sharply dressed young Greek men who accosted me were probably waiters or tour bus drivers during the day, but at this time of night they were gentlemen of leisure, lavish with their offers of hospitality. But I was no longer as innocent as I had been when I came to Greece: I knew that friendliness would be interpreted as willingness, and accepting hospitality could lead to an undignified wrestling match later in the evening as your host tried to collect on his investment.

One young man with excellent English was very persistent. "I've seen the Acropolis," I told him, and his delighted laugh told me that he'd read the very funny book about foreign girls and Greek men *Excuse Me Miss, Have You Seen the Acropolis?*

"Come on, all Greek men aren't like that," he said. "Give me a chance to prove it to you." He was really good-looking, dark and slender with a humorous glint in his brown eyes, and I was tempted. But I reminded myself that I was in Delphi to work, not to play, and I shook my head with a laugh.

"Some other time perhaps," I said diplomatically. "I'm really tired tonight." He looked at me appraisingly and decided that I really meant it.

"Some other time, but soon," he said cheerfully. "I'll be looking for you; my name is Nikos." He said something in rapid Greek to the little group of young men he was with, and they strolled away with a few backward glances and more conversation too rapid for me to catch much. I went back to my little room feeling irrationally disappointed that he'd taken me at my word.

The next morning I was up early and spent most of breakfast answering Kyria Amalia's questions or evading them when they got too personal. At last I got away from her and hurried down the village street to the site enclosing the ruins of the Temple of Apollo and the surrounding buildings, getting there a good hour early. No one was around, and the gate was firmly locked. I remembered that the pilgrims to Delphi in the old days had washed themselves in the Castalian Spring as a preparation for their visit to the shrine, so I followed the sign that pointed down the road and came to the great cleft in the cliffs where the water of the spring trickles down from the mountain. I knelt by the channel where the water ran, cupped my hands, and drank deeply of the deliciously cold water: once, twice, three times. Then I splashed water on my face and bathed my wrists, a ritual three times each. If anyone had been watching me, I might have felt silly, but there was a need in me to mark the beginning of my visit to the shrine with some kind of ceremony.

I walked slowly back to the site, feeling in the right mood to appreciate it now and wishing that I didn't have most of an hour to wait. When I got to the gate, though, it was open, and there was no one to be seen. A broom was leaning against the fence, and a little pile of rubbish was near it; it looked as if a guard who'd been tidying up had gone off for a dustpan. I looked at the completely deserted ruins inside the gate and was suddenly tempted. It wasn't as if I were slipping in without paying. I had my pass. And I had been on so many archaeological sites where the incongruous crowds of tourists had kept me from really drinking in the history and beauty of the place. I gave in to temptation, slipped in the gate, and hurried up the path to where I couldn't be seen from the gate.

I walked slowly along the path that climbed the steep hillside, trying to identify the buildings around me from the various guidebooks I'd read in preparation for the trip. At first there was just a jumble of ruins; then I saw the sturdily beautiful little building like a miniature temple that had housed the offerings to the god made by the Athenian people. The massive ruin higher up the hill must be the Temple. That big gray rock with the deep cleft in it which was just beyond the little building must be the Rock of Sibyl, where the Delphic oracle had begun. *Sibyl* is an ancient word for a female prophet, and some stories said that the first oracle had been a priestess of the earth goddess. Other legends said that a shepherd had inhaled some kind of underground vapors here and begun to babble prophecies.

Suddenly I stopped and stared in amazement. As I stood there in the bright sunlight of the twentieth century, something like mist or smoke was rising from around the Rock of Sibyl, thickening and gathering until the rock was almost hidden! I told myself that I must be hallucinating, that all the books said that the vapors were only a legend. No one had ever found any underground source from which such vapors could come. Perhaps workmen on the site were burning off some brush or perhaps . . . what? I couldn't think of any other plausible explanation, and I knew that this really couldn't be smoke; there was no sound or smell of burning. Excitement tingled through me as I realized that if this wasn't a hallucination— if it was real—I might have stumbled across something that might help explain one of the great mysteries of ancient Delphi. Even though it was pure accident, I could be famous for blundering into this phenomenon.

But what if it vanished, leaving me only with a story no one would believe? If I could just capture some of the vapor in some kind of container, perhaps it could be analyzed. I fumbled frantically in my daypack and brought out my water bottle, which I had just filled at the spring. With fingers made clumsy by haste, I got the cap off and spilled out the water; it seemed to take ages to empty. Now if I could just collect some of the vapor without breathing any . . . I edged cautiously toward the vapor, but it seemed to recede in front of me. I thought of the dream rushes in *Through the Looking Glass*. Didn't they vanish as Alice tried to gather them? Or was it after she had got them in the boat?

I looked to each side of me to see if the mist was thicker there.

It was—much thicker. My breath caught in my throat as I realized that the mist was like a wall on each side of me, cutting out my view of everything around me. I whirled around and saw that I was trapped in a shadowy tunnel formed by the mists, a tunnel which was closing in behind me but seemed now to be stretching far ahead!

I felt a deep reluctance to touch those misty walls or let myself be touched by the mists crowding in behind. I began to walk slowly ahead, and I could tell that I was going uphill from the feel of the ground beneath my feet. After a few moments I realized that something was wrong. If I were going in the direction I thought I was, I would have run into the massive retaining wall of the Temple. Even if I had got myself turned around somehow, I surely couldn't have gone this far without running into one or another of the ruins. The misty tunnel looked perfectly straight, but I wondered what would happen if I turned right or left. Would the walls retreat before me as the original mist had? What if I turned around and tried to walk back the way I had come?

I had nearly made up my mind to try it when ahead of me I saw a gray mass of stone and behind it what seemed to be a break in the mist. After even a few moments in the tunnel of mist I had a frantic desire for any way out into the world of ordinary shapes and colors. I rushed ahead to the great gray boulder, and when I saw grass and flowers growing from the small crevices in it, I put my hands out to hold the rock in what was almost an embrace.

Instantly the mists vanished, and I was again in the bright sunshine. Above me soared the great cliffs, the Shining Ones. I turned and looked in the direction from which I had come, or seemed to come. The Rock of Sibyl was not far away from me, down a grassy slope; I could have thrown the water bottle I still held and hit it easily. I must be, could only be on the great platform on which the Temple stood. But around me and below me were no ruins, no buildings of any sort, no road. I stood in a place which had not a single trace of the great shrine of Delphi!

# CHAPTER TWO

At first I grasped at obvious explanations. My first thought was that I must have blacked out somehow and wandered away to some deserted hillside near the shrine. But as I stood and looked around me, I felt a chilling certainty that this could not be true. The line of the cliffs above me, the look of the hills across the great valley, everything about the hillside *except* for the ruins were identical to what I had been looking at before the mists rose around the Rock of Sibyl. Even the Rock itself, deceptively innocent in the bright sun, with no wisp of mist around it, was the same.

As I looked frantically around me, I began to see little differences. The valley floor was a different color, greener somehow. The cliffs, even the Rock of Sibyl itself seemed . . . *newer* . . . less crumbled and weathered. But instead of making me less sure that I was in the same place I had been before the mists arose, it perversely made me surer. I had not moved in space, not in any ordinary way. This was Delphi; this was the site of the shrine; that was the Rock of Sibyl. Only the works of human hands had vanished.

I took my hands from the rock and tried to calm myself by breathing deeply and slowly. All right, if this was really happening, if it wasn't a dream or a hallucination, then I was in a way prepared for it. Unlike Eustace Scrubb in *The Voyage of the Dawn Treader*, I *had* read the right books—the ones in which someone from our world is snatched away by science or magic to another world or another time: to Narnia, to Oz; to the prehistoric past or the distant future. I was sure that this was not a dream or a hallucination; it was too solid, too . . . *everyday*. The sun was hot on my head and arms and back; there was a twig or pebble in my sandal. Birds sang in the trees nearby, and a faint breeze rustled the long grass at my feet. This world around me was real, but what reality was it?

Something niggled at my mind. What had seemed strange when I thought of the stone in my sandal? Why, the sandal itself. Surely I'd put on hiking shoes this morning for scrambling around the rocky site, not sandals of scuffed dark leather tied to my feet with leather thongs. I didn't even own such a pair of sandals. And the coarse material on my legs was not the cloth of my jeans, but the skirt of some sort of dress, tied at my waist with a cord. I lifted the water bottle I held in my hand. It had been a plastic bike water bottle, smaller and handier to carry in my daypack than a full-size canteen. But now it was a gracefully shaped vessel of clay with a stopper that looked like wood, dangling from the vessel by a leather thong.

My certainty that this all was real wavered, then returned. If the site had changed around me, why shouldn't small things like my clothing and my water bottle change too? Had *I* changed in some way? I looked at my hands and arms, then down at my feet. They didn't *seem* different from the hands and arms and feet that I was used to seeing. I grabbed a hunk of my hair and discovered that it was longer than it had been—loose, rather than in the braid I had made that morning. But the color seemed the same, and the texture. If I had a mirror or some substitute for one, I could see if my face was the same, but I had a feeling that it was.

I took a step away from the rock I had been holding on to, then hesitated. If I left this place, would it make it harder to get home, back to my own world? Then I clenched my teeth and continued walking. Since I didn't have the faintest idea of how I'd gotten here, it was no use clinging to this rock and waiting for something to happen. I might as well explore this world I found myself in.

Since I didn't have any idea which way to go, I took the path of least resistance and followed the slope of the hill downward until I stood just above the Rock of Sibyl. It looked completely ordinary, but I was strangely reluctant to touch it. I kept a little distance away as I picked my way down the steeper slope here to the level where in the place or time I had been in so short a while ago a paved path led past the Rock up to the great Temple. I stopped and stared, feelings of mingled joy and fear pulsing through me.

I could see now what I had not noticed from higher up the slope: that a faint trail led up to the base of the Rock and stopped there. And at the base of the Rock itself, hidden from the slope above, was a little platform of wood on which there stood beautiful little vessels of clay, shaped like shallow bowls. I was not alone here, wherever here was. There were human beings—or at least beings—here who could shape and bake clay to make things both useful and beautiful.

I knelt in front of the little platform and looked into the clay vessels. One held some kind of grain, smaller and darker than wheat—barley perhaps? Another held a clear amber substance. I tentatively poked at it with my finger. Sticky. A little fearfully I licked that finger—honey. The liquid in another bowl looked like milk. Milk and honey—and grain. I suddenly realized how dry my tongue and mouth were, from fear and from exertion in the hot sun. The milk, sheltered by the shade of the rock from the burning sun, might still be good. I lifted the bowl and breathed in the rich smell of fresh milk, put my lips to the brim of the bowl, and let the cool liquid touch my lips. The temptation was too great. I tilted up the bowl and drank until it was dry, then put it down gently. It would serve me right if the milk were drugged or poisoned, but that cool draft had seemed worth the risk. Still, it had been a foolish thing to do. I had better . . .

"Beware." For a moment I didn't realize that the voice had spoken outside my mind. Once I did, I was on my feet and turning to look behind me in one startled movement. At what I saw I could only stand and stare.

The woman who stood there was a little shorter than I am, but as I looked into her dark eyes, I felt like a child who had been up to mischief. She wore a long dark dress—no, robe. Her feet were bare, but her black hair was combed and braided into an intricate and elaborate hairdo. She looked a little like Kyria Amalia, a little like the mother superior at my old parochial school, a little like . . . Like a goddess, I said to myself. I've never seen a goddess, but this is what a goddess might look like.

"The milk is for our Mother, girl, not for a thirsty child," she said in a voice that was kind but stern. I felt just as I had when I had been called to Mother Superior's office to answer for some childish infraction of the rules at the school. Physically she was quite unlike Mother Superior, I realized, but she had the same air of quiet authority, of complete certainty, of dedication. With a veil and wimple around it, her face could easily be the face of one of the older nuns who, dressed in their traditional habits, had seemed to us children another race of beings, perhaps lower than the angels but high above mere humans.

"Where did you come from, child?" the woman asked, and I found myself answering with automatic deference, "From the village, Mother. Before that from Athens. And—"

She frowned and said sharply, "Athens? In Attica? How did you come such a distance?"

"In a tour bus, Mother," I said, but even as I said the words, I felt that there was something absurd about them. *Tour bus*—strange words, meaningless words.

The woman's puzzled expression may have given me that feeling, for very evidently my words meant nothing to her. For a moment she seemed angry; then she looked at me sharply and said, "Did you come to visit the shrine, child?" Her tone was gentler, but it was as if she were speaking to a small child rather than to an adult.

"Oh, yes," I said, a little off-balance and overtalkative. "The great shrine of Apollo, the Temple—"

"Apollo!" Her voice showed puzzlement and a touch of contempt. "This is our Mother's place, and I am Her priestess. The son of Leto stole Her shrine on the Holy Island, but he has no place here, and certainly no temple!"

"There will be a temple and much else," came a voice from above me. I whirled around again and saw that a young man was standing on the Rock, his gold-trimmed sandals above the level of our heads. He wore a simple white tunic, but his hair was bound with a band and fell in curls which seemed too regular and artificial to be natural. Perhaps it was his stance above us or perhaps it was the more than human calm and authority that seemed to emanate from his face, but I had the curious feeling that his body should be made of bronze or stone rather than of smoothly tanned flesh. It was a shock when he sprang down from the Rock with the grace of an athlete and stood between me and the priestess.

"In times to come this hill will be covered with temples and trophies dedicated to the son of Zeus and Leto," he said to the woman. I was still trying to come to terms with his words *in times to come* when he turned to me. His brilliant blue eyes seemed to see into my mind, and he said with a little smile that frightened rather than reassured me, "Yes, girl, the Path you walked led you back to what for you is the distant past. You were called here to give witness. Tell her of the temples, the pilgrims, the other glories of Apollo's shrine."

I stumbled into speech, hardly knowing what I was saying. "The—the great Temple of Apollo is up there." I gestured to the place where I had emerged from what this strange young man had called the Path. "And above are the theater and the stadium . . . people come from all over the world." For some reason there was a twitch of annoyance on the man's face when I mentioned the theater. I wondered what his reaction would be if I went on to say that everything was in ruins and it was tourists, not pilgrims, who came in my day to Apollo's shrine. A sound like the hiss of a snake came from the woman's lips, seeming to express both anger and disbelief.

"The girl babbles meaningless words," she said, "and even if some Olympian trickery has drawn her from a place where these things are true, that only shows what *may* be, not what *will* be. Leto's son will never be honored on this mountain while the Guardian of the Shrine lives."

There was a deadly coldness in the young stranger's voice, and I was glad that those coldly brilliant eyes were not fixed on me as he said, "If a death is necessary, a death there will be. Only a fool, though, goes to battle when defeat is certain. Make your peace with Apollo while you can, priestess of Rhea, and your Lady will always have her shrine and her due honor in Apollo's precincts. Resist me, and I will cast her out."

The sneering laugh with which the priestess answered this threat made my knees grow almost too weak to hold me up. She no longer reminded me in the least of Mother Superior. Her eyes seemed to flash dark fire as she replied, "Cast *Her* out! Before Her you are almost as much a baby, a creature of the day, as this mortal child. Run away, little Olympian, and forget your dreams of temples and trophies on this holy mountain. My Lady rules here and will always rule. If the Lines of Time seem to point at a shrine here for you, She will take them in Her hands and form them anew. This poor little ghost from time to come will vanish away, along with your temples and trophies, when her world vanishes."

I almost felt that the power the woman served could do just that: annihilate, abolish not only me but my world. I felt like Alice, not believing that she was "only a thing in his dream" but still afraid to wake the Red King. Yet the young stranger's voice was calm, almost indifferent as he said, "So she might if I left her in possession of the Gates and Powers of this place. Nor would I lightly pit myself against my father's mother. But it is not she that I face, priestess, but only you. The Old Gods are far away from their servants now; their day is done. The Olympians need this place and its power. *I* need it. I claim it in my father's name and in my own name, I, Apollo, Leto's son and son of Zeus."

My knees gave way entirely, and I slid down till I was crouching against the base of the Rock. This *must* be, it *had* to be a dream or delirium. How could I be here in the clear light of day and hear a slender young man name himself as the god Apollo without feeling the slightest doubt that he was speaking the truth? Apollo was only a myth, only a legend. But my own mind answered me: only a myth in my day—but this was not my day.

The priestess laughed a deep, full-throated laugh with what seemed to be genuine amusement in it. "*Only* me to fight, little godling?" she sneered. "Did you expect an easy victory against some poor mortal creature with only borrowed powers? Fool and upstart, my Lady did not leave this place lightly guarded. I am the Pythia, of the blood of the Old Ones, and I am your doom!"

Suddenly her dark form was no longer that of a woman; where the woman's figure had stood was the monstrous head of a serpent, whose giant body sprawled down the slopes, long as a train and nearly as bulky. I couldn't tear my gaze away when that head rose higher and higher in the air and the great mouth gaped open, but I gave a little moan and shrank back against the Rock as that monstrous bulk rose and towered above us, blocking out the sun, ready to fall and annihilate not only me but my whole world.

"Peace, little mortal," came the calm, beautiful voice of the young stranger who had called himself Apollo. "I did not bring you here to feed you to the Pythia." Incredibly there was a hint of laughter in that voice. I wrenched my eyes from the giant serpent, and my breath caught when I saw that in the gloom of the serpent's horrible shadow Apollo's flesh glowed faintly with a golden light. He made a gesture with his hand as if he were reaching for something, but there was a strange feeling in my eyes when I tried to follow the direction of that reach, a wrenching feeling as if I had made some impossible demand on my merely mortal eyes.

Now there was something in the young god's left hand, a thing like a streak of silvery light but shaped like a bow. The names echoed in my mind from the poets: Apollo the Archer, Apollo of the Silver Bow. His right hand came up and seemed to draw a bowstring; a thin streak of light, intolerably bright, sprang from his fingers and crossed the bow of light. The bow was drawn, the arrow in place. Apollo looked up as if to parley one last time with his monstrous opponent, but the gigantic head was already beginning its descent. Instantly the fingers of his right hand opened, and that streak of brilliance flew like the arrow it seemed to be, straight at the monstrous head.

As the arrow flew through the air, it left a trail of light that lengthened until it touched the Rock above my head. The fiery dart tore through the serpent's head and continued on into the sky, leaving its trail, an arc of fire that seemed to reach to the hills across the valley.

When the fiery arrow pierced the great snake's head, it gave a terrible shriek that made me clap my hands to my ears. That line of fire did not fade but seemed to hold the serpent like a fish strung on a line. The body spasmed, the great tail beat the ground, but the head was hooked immovably on that line of light.

A singing sound seemed to come from the arc of fire, so loud that I heard it though my hands were still over my ears. I looked to see that the line of light now reached far behind me, up the slope, skimming above the rock which stood where the Temple would stand, reaching on up the hill until it touched the cliffs above. But while I watched, the line of light died, and the singing sound died with it. I took my hands from my ears and caught the last dying whisper of the sound. The serpent's shrieks had ceased, and when I turned again, there was nothing left of that terrifying shape but a small dark bundle on the ground.

Apollo bent and lifted the bundle in his arms with incongruous tenderness; he might have been lifting the body of a dead lover. When he came back to me with the body in his arms, I could see the face of the priestess, her head lolled against his shoulder. In death her face had regained its nobility and peace. He laid the body down and looked at it.

"She was part mortal after all," said Apollo, a tinge of sadness beneath the calm of his voice. "If she had been an Old One, she would not have died, only would have been held there powerless until I released her. But I didn't know and couldn't take a chance. I had to send the full power of the Path through her body; only that would have stopped one of the Old Ones. But this poor half mortal died by that which she was set to guard."

The god's cold eyes looked over the body of his victim at me. "She would never have stood on a Line of Power with me between her and a gate if I had come alone," he said almost to himself. "You were of use after all, though she would not hear your witness," he said musingly, his eyes more aware of me now.

Hysteria rose in me, and I found myself shouting at him, shrieking at him, "You used me, you *used* me to trap her and distract her. You used me to help you murder her." For the moment I had forgotten the monstrous serpent and saw only the nobility of the dead face.

"Yes," said the god simply. "I did. It was necessary, and it was for the good of your mortal kind, in ways you can hardly understand. But you are right, it was murder, and I will have to pay a price for it. And it is true that I have used you without your consent; there is a price to be paid for that too. We are bound together, you and I, in debt and guilt. I can be free of you, and you of me, but only at a price."

I stared at him, filled with conflicting fears. I was afraid of further involvement yet afraid, too, that I would be expelled from this new world of wonders now that he had made use of me. One bigger fear moved me to speech: "Could she really have changed history— made my world . . . disappear?"

He shook his head. "She, the priestess? No. Her mistress perhaps has the power, but I think not even she would dare make so great a change without knowing what would come of it. Of all the immortals, I see what is to come most clearly, and when I act to change what is to come, I confuse my own vision for a while. The greater the change, the less I can see, and the longer it takes for my vision to clear. And the greater the change, the harder it is to make the Stream resist change."

"The Stream?" I asked, wondering why he was telling me all this.

He shrugged. "It is what I call it in my own thoughts. There are few I can speak of these things to." He took me by the arm and walked me over to a little stream that ran down the slope. My arm seemed to tingle a little where his fingers touched me, a disconcerting sensation but not unpleasant. He pointed at the rivulet. "I think of Time as like that stream," he said. "We are like specks being carried along on the stream. See the water bug there? It can run along the stream, faster than the current or against it. It can pick up a speck and carry it back and forth with it. The specks are immersed in the stream and have no way of knowing where it will carry them; the bug can stand a little above the water and see at least the large things ahead of it. But it can do little to change the course of the stream. A larger creature, more powerful, could do more."

He bent over and with amazing ease picked up a large boulder and laid it in the streambed, damming the rivulet. Water boiled up around the stone and began to flow out of the channel, trickling along the ground, seeking alternate paths down the hill. Eventually most of the water found its way back into the original streambed, and a few yards downhill the stream was back to its normal course despite the dam.

"It flows where it flowed before, because the ground is as it is and because of the weight of the water from above," he said. "But see how the water boils around the rock and finds its way in many little paths below the dam I have made. Until the water creates a new channel, it would be very hard to know how one speck will go. Yet before I blocked the stream, it would have been easy to say just how a speck would travel over that stretch of the stream."

"I'm not a speck in the Stream of Time," I said, annoyed by his words. "I'm free."

He smiled. "Think of yourself as a feebler water bug then, not strong enough to fight the current but able to move somewhat on the stream. Yes, even mortals are free, and yet even immortals are limited in what they can do. To be completely free, you would have to be all-powerful, subject to no limitations."

"But an all-powerful being could even change Time," I said, trying to puzzle it out.

He shrugged. "It lies in the meaning of the words. I am far from being all-powerful, but what I can see and reach I can change, to the limit of my powers. If my power had no limits . . . Well, it has many, yet I could reach out and bring you here."

"Why me?" I asked, trying to meet his eyes with mine. After a moment I had to look away.

He smiled again, that far from comforting smile. "I did not send for you by name, girl; even my powers cannot see individuals very far off in times to come, only the big things, the things as hard to change as the course of a stream. I sent out a call through the Path, to draw one who could testify to things to come, one with the strength to make the journey and not be broken by it. And if the Pythia had not been a fool, it would have worked. She would have heard you and realized that a shrine for me here bulked too large in times to come for her to change. She should have seen that it was no use to fight. I would not have had to kill her and take the consequences of killing her."

Suddenly my mind made a connection, and I gasped as if I had been doused with cold water. "The legends . . ." I began in so small a voice that I had to begin again. "The legends say that Apollo killed the Pythian serpent and took the shrine for his own. But for killing the serpent he was punished by the gods. . . ."

He gave a bitter little laugh. "Yes. And do your stories say that the Great Olympians will send me for a year to serve as a shepherd, a shepherd to a mortal king? I have not avoided that, and cannot now. Yet the Great Olympians will make use of what I have gained here, even while I serve out my slavery to a mortal. A year—"

Rightly or wrongly I heard self-pity in his voice, and I thought again of the dead priestess. "What is a year to an immortal?" I snapped.

His strangely brilliant eyes sought mine, and this time I could not turn my eyes away. "What is a year to an immortal?" he repeated softly. "Why, perhaps only like a day to a mortal. A small thing— or is it? They will take a year from me, girl; well, I will take a day from you. Only a day—from a sleep to a sleep . . ."

As he said "sleep" for the second time, a horrible drowsiness overcame me. My whole body seemed drowned with sleep, buried in sleep. Only for a moment before I lost consciousness entirely I could still see those blue eyes blazing into mine. . . .

# CHAPTER THREE

"Wake up, you worthless brat." The harsh voice was accompanied by a horny hand, which picked me up by the scruff of the neck and hurled me out of the pile of tattered fleeces that had been my bed. The few bars of pale sunlight that penetrated the hut told me the sun was already up, but huddled lumps under some of the fleeces showed that others were still asleep. I rubbed sleep out of my eyes as I crouched on the floor of beaten earth, gagging a little at the frowsty smell of too many unwashed bodies huddled too close. The hulking figure of the man who had dragged me out of bed loomed over me, thrusting a leather bucket at me.

"Get some water up here quick, and whatever sticks you can find for the fire," the man growled, and a push from his foot propelled me through the fleece which covered the low door of the hut. I stood in a rocky little valley which might have been anywhere. A little stream ran a stone's throw away, and I stumbled over to it, dragging the bucket. The frost on the grass was melting, but it was still bitterly cold on my bare feet. I tried to huddle into my cloak, but it was too threadbare to offer much warmth. I filled the bucket at a place where the bed of the stream had been crudely dug out to make a little pool, then knelt by the pool and shivered for a moment. I took water in my hands and splashed it on my face, once, twice, three times, wondering why that stirred some dim memory.

More awake now, I peered around me in the cold light of early morning. The ground this side of the stream was bare, but across it I saw a scrawny bush with some dead branches. Wading through the icy stream was agonizing, but once across, I was able to break

off enough dead branches to make a fair-size bundle. I endured the
icy wade again and struggled back to the hut, the heavy bucket of
water in one hand, the awkward bundle of sticks under my other
arm.

The big man who had aroused me was in front of the hut, blowing
vigorously on the ashes of last night's fire. He grunted at me as I
approached and reached out a hand for my sticks. I put down the
bucket, dropped the sticks at his feet, and held out some smaller
twigs to him. He gave a friendlier grunt, took the twigs, and thrust
them into the coals. As they caught, he piled the larger sticks on
top until he had a small blaze going. You could hardly see the
flames in the strengthening sun, but the warmth of the fire was
very welcome on my cold legs. The man poured some water from
the bucket into a fire-blackened clay pot and put it close to the
flames. Then he went into the hut, leaving me to warm myself at
the fire.

I heard him bawling at the others and their answering groans
and curses. By the time they emerged, blinking and tousled, the
big man had brought out a little crudely carved wooden box and
from it had thrown a handful of what looked like dry leaves into
the now steaming pot of water.

"Mountain tea," he said gruffly. "If you'd rather have the dregs
of last night's wine with your bread, that's your lookout, but water
it well. You'll need your wits about you this morning. We're taking
the flock down the hill. I'll tell you again what I told you last
night; you probably drank it out of your heads. I'm Iaptos, the
king's chief shepherd, not that that means much. So far as I'm
concerned, you're just three outland shepherds, no matter what
crazy tales the diviners have told the king. The gods know I can
use men who know one end of a sheep from another, but I've no
use for mountebanks and tricksters. Do a decent day's work, and
there'll be an occasional skin of wine, like last night, and a bit of
lamb now and again that the palace won't miss. As for you, brat,
make yourself useful when you can and keep out of the way when
you can't. Here."

He broke off a hunk of hard bread from a loaf under his arm and
dipped some of the steaming tea into a cracked mug. He thrust
these at me, then tossed the loaf to a tall man and dipped himself

some tea. The man followed Iaptos' example, but the other two shared the last dribbles of wine from a flaccid wineskin. The thin man with the discontented mouth watered the wine, but his stocky, full-bearded companion drank his neat, ignoring the chief shepherd's advice.

Iaptos leaned across the fire and picked up the water bucket. With one easy motion he dashed the remaining water in the stocky man's face. The man spluttered and sprang to his feet, fists clenched, but his eyes dropped before the steady gaze of the formidable Iaptos, and he turned away, cursing. "If you won't take it inside, you'll take it outside," said Iaptos with a chuckle. "Here, brat, fill this bucket again and start swilling out that pigpen in there. Haul the fleeces out, and air them till just before we leave. You three start getting the sheep together."

For the rest of the day I did a great deal more making myself useful than keeping out of the way. I cleaned the hut. I packed the few things that we took from the hut and carried them too. I trudged after the flock as it made its slow way down the hills, kept together by the three shepherds and the dogs. Except for occasionally shouting a direction, Iaptos let them do the work and merely strode along with his staff. But when I began to stumble and falter late in the afternoon, he took the pack from my back and slung it over his own shoulder. Even so, when we reached our destination as the shadows of evening fell, I was staggering with weariness.

He let me collapse for a while as the shepherds penned the sheep in a rough stockade, but then he sent me off for wood and water again; luckily here at this prepared camp in the lowlands there was a pile of cut wood and a cistern for water not far from the hut.

I was half asleep by the fire after wolfing down my share of a greasy stew when there was a sudden stir. Iaptos and the others rose respectfully to their feet, and when I was slow to do the same, I was hauled to mine. A slender young woman in a white robe stood before us. There was a gleam of gold at her wrists and throat, and the gesture with which she waved us back to our seats was quietly authoritative. I hardly needed the murmur of "my Queen" from Iaptos to know her for what she was.

She looked across the fire at the weather-beaten faces of the three shepherds with something in her eyes that might have been desperation. "I am Alcestis, Lady of Pherae," she said. "My husband, Admetos, the King of Pherae, is a favorite of Apollo; he told me himself that Apollo helped him pass the test my father set to weed out suitors for my hand. Admetos is ill—very ill—and I thought that Apollo had abandoned him. But now the wise men claim to have received a message from the gods. They say that Apollo will live among us for a year, in the guise of a mortal; that one of you who crossed our borders three days ago is Apollo himself!"

Iaptos gave a snort of disbelief and spoke up. "With all respect, Lady," he said, "I think your wise men must have made a mistake. I've never met these three until I met them at the border of our land, but if any of them is a god, I'm a ewe lamb. I'm not saying that they're ordinary shepherds because they're not. The tall one there can cure diseases in people as well as animals; he cured a burn on my hand and healed a sick lamb when we first met. But night before last there was a child ill in a village near where we harbored. This man wouldn't get up out of his bed and walk over the hill to the village to see what he could do for her. No thanks to him she didn't die. What kind of god would that be who wouldn't help a dying child?"

Iaptos scowled at the tall shepherd and then turned his glare on the thin man who had watered his wine that morning. "This skinny one can harp and sing so well you forget your troubles. But it doesn't make him forget his. You can tell it's just a job with him and one he's weary of; he claims that's why he wants to go back to being a shepherd, as he was when he was young. Would the god of music and poetry find his own art wearisome?"

Iaptos turned an even fiercer scowl on the bearded man who had drunk his wine unmixed that morning. "This sot here is too fond of his wine to be good for much," Iaptos growled, "but he has a little bag of tricks: He can make noises and lights appear in unexpected places; he can change the look of things so that they appear to be something else. But he's no god; his wonders are no use to anyone and mean nothing. Surely a god is something more than a trickster."

Alcestis lifted her hand to silence Iaptos. "Peace, old friend," she said. "You won't convince me that the god isn't one among these men, only that he hides himself cleverly, pretending to be a

freak and surrounding himself with other freaks. It's easier to minimize your powers than hide them altogether. Apollo is wise enough
to know that even disguised, he'd stand out among ordinary mortals.
But I know the god is here, and I have no need to know which
one he is, only to know he hears me. Lord Apollo, if you ever loved
my husband, please, please heal him now. Every day he grows
weaker. . . ."

The three shepherds hung their heads and shuffled their feet,
embarrassed by the naked pleading in the queen's voice. Iaptos
looked ready to burst with indignation at seeing his queen abase
herself before men he regarded as impostors. The queen gave a little
half sob that seemed to wake my mind from a sort of stupor it had
been in all day as I stumbled from task to task, weary, cold, and
confused.

"Alcestis," I said, "your husband will die unless someone freely
offers to die in his place." It wasn't until startled eyes sought my
face that I realized that I had spoken aloud. What could I say if
she asked me how I knew? Tell her that I was half remembering a
play by Euripides, a play based on a legend about Alcestis, Queen
of Pherae?

Iaptos growled indignantly and would have spoken, but the queen
stopped him with a frown. "Quiet, Iaptos," she said sternly, "the
god has kept his identity hidden and answered me through the
mouth of this child. My place is to find someone who is willing to
offer his life for my husband. He is a great and good king, much
beloved. Surely it will not be hard. And when I have found someone,
the god will take him and save my husband. Thank you, thank
you, my Lord!" She turned and walked out of the circle of firelight
and walked away; I heard the click of her bracelets and then the
clatter of bronze armor as the escort who had been waiting for her
fell in behind her.

Iaptos turned on me, his eyes blazing. "Curse you, brat, if you're
lying," he thundered, "and curse you twenty times more if you
told the truth. No one loves King Admetos well enough to die for
him, not his friends, not even his parents, no one except Alcestis
herself. She's worth a hundred of him, but she'd lay down her life
for him, and he, the self-infatuated fool, he would let her! Agh,
what am I tormenting myself for. The god of death doesn't take

substitutes; you're mad or mountebanks, all of you! Get to bed;
I'm banking this fire. Tomorrow we'll work the nonsense out of
your heads!"

All of us huddled under our sheepskins to escape the big man's
wrath, flinching as he slammed clods on the fire to bank the coals.
For a while the excitement of what had happened kept me awake,
but then the exhaustion of the day began to overcome me. Only as
I peered around the hut before falling into sleep, I saw in a vagrant
gleam of firelight a face turned toward me, the face of one of the
shepherds huddled under his sheepskins. And from that shadowy
face, anonymous in the gloom, two brilliant blue eyes met mine.

# CHAPTER FOUR

I awoke on the hillside with the god standing before me and the huddled body of the priestess at our feet. "You used me again," I stormed at him, "used me to give that magnificent woman that awful choice—while you hid yourself!"

He met my angry gaze with his mirthless smile. "Not *used*," he said. "What you experienced did not really happen and will not happen; it is only a shadow of what might be, a dream if you like. It will not be you I use, though there may be a shepherd's lad I *can* use. And the mortal guise will be not my choice but part of my punishment. Would you like to share the rest of that year with me?"

"No," I admitted. "It was hard enough for me. I can see what it would mean to—someone used to being . . . what you are. Which one were you?" I went on hurriedly.

I could see from his smile he did not mean to answer. "I think the tall, silent one," I said. "He didn't go to the child, but it was dying and it didn't die. You wouldn't need to be there to help her, would you?"

"Perhaps not," he said impassively. "But perhaps both you and Iaptos assume too easily that a god will always help when asked for help. Do the gods you pray to always grant what you ask?"

"The God I pray to, when he was on earth as a mortal, always healed those who asked him," I said. He looked at me with a puzzled frown.

"There's no tale I know of any of the Olympians or the Old Gods that matches that," he said. "But of course, you're from times to come—some new god, perhaps. By the beard of Kronos, how far did I call you from? How long ago in your time is . . . what would your folk remember? Do they remember the island near Crete that was destroyed by a fire mountain?"

"Yes, we know of that," I told him. "By our reckoning, it was . . . let's see, fourteen and nineteen . . . about thirty-three hundred years ago in my time."

At last I had made an impression on him; there was consternation in those cold blue eyes. "So long," he almost whispered. "So long. From across the Divide that not even the Great Olympians see beyond. Are we even remembered, girl, Zeus and his brethren and children?"

"Remembered," I told him, "but no longer worshiped."

He didn't seem to be much disturbed by this. "We Olympians know that our day will not last forever. Before us were the Old Gods, and they did not foresee us; but they knew their day was not forever either. We know our time will come but not how or what form the new gods will take. But you pose a problem, girl, coming from so far away in time."

A sudden stab of panic shot through me. "You mean that you can't get me back to my own time?"

His smile this time was a little more reassuring. "Don't fear, little one," he said. "The Path will return you to the time you came from. The problem will be to keep you there."

Mingled hope and fear shook me. "What do you mean, keep me there?" I asked.

He frowned thoughtfully. "It is not easy to explain to a mortal—not easy to find words for it all. It takes power to traverse a Path; it was my power that drew you here. But some of the power stays in you, and the Path may open for you again . . . and again. If you turn away from the Path when it opens, I think in time it will cease to open. If you go down it again, you would not come so far from your own time. Perhaps each time you would travel a shorter way from your own time, though it is not wise to rely on the Path's acting in a set way."

"You mean," I said slowly, "that I could step into those mists again and come out at other times, see the shrine as it was at different times in its history?"

He looked at me keenly. "This pleases you, I see. Why?" The

thought crossed my mind that he could see some things in my mind but not everything.

I tried to think of a way to answer him that he could understand. "In my own time I'm a student—one who is learning. I'm trying to learn about the past so that someday I can teach others. I came to Delphi to study its history—it's what we call a research project. . . ." The words sounded strange in my own ears, and I asked him, "Does any of this make sense to you?"

He gave a little laugh, the first I had heard from him. "To a man only of this time it would be hard to explain, yes," he said. "But I can look at things to come and at some of the pictures in your mind and understand a little. The world is too new now for its folk to look backward with much interest, but I can see that in time to come, some will make stories of the days gone by and others will try to find the truth about those days. And you think that among those who can only hunt among tales and relics you will be like one who has sight among the blind, for you will have seen these things. Perhaps you are right, and perhaps not. It can be a disadvantage to see too clearly."

I had opened my mouth to ask him what he meant when I suddenly became conscious of a strange odor, sickly sweet and disgusting. It seemed to come from the body of the dead priestess. Surely her flesh could not be decaying so rapidly! As I looked at the body for an instant, it seemed to blur and become a serpent's head with blank, dead eyes and gaping mouth. Out of the corner of my eye I seemed to see shadowy coils sprawling down the hill, but when I looked directly at them, they vanished.

Apollo could smell the odor too; his aristocratic nose was wrinkled fastidiously, but his face showed concern as well as disgust. "Time to get you out of here, girl," he said somberly. "The Powers that dwelt in the priestess are departing from her; it is not a safe place for mortals. I do not think that anything can follow you through the Path, but it is well to leave quickly before what dwelt in the woman is entirely free of her. Come."

There was that tingling touch on my arm again, and he led me up the slope to the rock I had touched when I emerged from the Path. "Others with greater power may enter the Path elsewhere along the Line of Power," he told me. "But for you it is probably necessary to enter at the two places where the Path comes closest to the world of mortals. Coming here, you entered at the Rock below and emerged here; you must now retrace your steps. Do not turn aside for anything; do not leave the Path until you again see clearly the Rock where we met. I will open the Path; go quickly."

There were a myriad of questions I would have liked to ask; but the smell was growing stronger, and I felt fidgety and uneasy. My body seemed to itch in odd places, and the hair on the back of my neck seemed to be bristling. When the mists formed about the rock, I took one last long look at the incredible reality of the slender young god and then plunged into the mists, which gave way before me.

At first the mists were as blank as before, but before I had gone very far, there seemed to a parting of the mist on my left hand; I could see sunlight, grass, and buildings of some kind. I hesitated and then went on, remembering Apollo's warning. The illusory opening in the mists vanished abruptly, and for a while there were only the mists. Then the mists ahead of me seemed to become the head of an enormous serpent with gaping mouth and dead eyes. The tunnel ahead of me seemed to lead directly down the throat of the monster!

Going on was the hardest thing I had ever done; without the memory of two brilliant blue eyes and the calm, beautiful voice of the god I could never have done it. Even so, I clenched my fists and closed my eyes as my steps seemed to take me beneath the monstrous fangs of the serpent. When I forced my eyes open a few steps farther on, the serpent form had vanished.

Surely I must have gone back as far as I had come on my first trip through the tunnel. Yes, there was the Rock of Sibyl! Or was it? It was off to the left of the path, not before me, and it seemed curiously insubstantial. I hesitated, then walked past the apparent rock, which vanished as abruptly as the sunlit scene had. A moment later I was rewarded by seeing the real Rock of Sibyl, solid and substantial, directly ahead of me, the mist thinning behind it. I touched the Rock, and the mists vanished.

I was standing on the upper side of the Rock, looking down the slope, and with tremendous relief I saw the Treasury of the Athenians on my right and the other ruins below me. The motor of a tour bus on the road below and a guard's whistle were sweet music to me at that moment. My clothing and water bottle were back to normal, but I wasn't wearing a watch. The site was still deserted, and I wondered if my trip through time had taken much of the time of my own world. But somehow I was sure it had not, and when I asked a friendly English tourist the time and date, I found it hadn't. She looked at me a little oddly, but I was too relieved to care.

Faced with the ordinary world, unchanged in any way from what it had been when the mists arose from the Rock, you might have thought that I would believe that the whole thing had been a dream or a hallucination. And there were times in the days to come when I did think just that, but never when I had just come from the Path. I knew then that what I had experienced on the other side of the mists was as real as anything I had experienced in my life.

I climbed down from the Rock and walked slowly along the stone path that led up to the Temple. At first the jumbled rocks around me seemed meaningless, but when I came around the corner and saw the great altar of Apollo towering above me, I felt a sudden thrill. The worship of Apollo had flourished here for hundreds of years, and even now throngs of people came from every part of the world to see the wreck of the grandeur that had been here.

When I came to the ruins of the Temple, I felt a sudden stab of interest. The rock where I had emerged from the tunnel must be here somewhere in the Temple itself. I walked up the ramp to the Temple entrance, then clambered along the uneven rocks that remained of the Temple floor. Roughly in the center of the Temple was a rough gray rock showing only its top among the foundations. But it was undoubtedly the top of the rock I had seen in the past. When this Temple was built, they must have filled in around the rock, perhaps even covered it up. But without any question it was the same rock.

The rest of the afternoon I wandered over the site, trying to fit the realities of the present to my fading but still vivid memories of what had happened beyond the mists. On that day the theater and the stadium meant very little to me; my trip had been to the past where they did not yet exist. I was fascinated by the hillside itself, and when I had looked at all the remaining ruins, I began the first of many explorations of the wilder parts of the site. I found a myriad of small trails and secluded nooks, many of them beautiful and fragrant with wildflowers and flowering shrubs. I think it was that first day when I followed a length of water pipe up the hill and found the little cistern that collected the water as it trickled down the hill from above.

When the guards cleared the site at three o'clock, I dawdled as much as I could, watching to see their procedures. I already had the feeling that I needed solitude if I was going to see the Path open to me again, a feeling that was to grow in the days to come. I could not count on an unattended gate again, and one way of having the site to myself was to hide and be left on the site when they locked it up. But the guards were depressingly thorough, and the vegetation on the hillside was sparse enough to make complete concealment difficult.

When at last I had to leave the site, I was reluctant to go back to my room and Kyria Amalia's clattering tongue. I turned the other way, away from town, at the gate and strolled along the road, trying to enjoy the view across the valley. But traffic was heavy as tour buses and cars carried people away from the site and museum. I was not enjoying my walk much, and when I saw steps going down the hill, I decided to see where they led.

It was only a short flight, and at the foot of the stairs was a charming little area filled with tables and chairs and roofed over with an arbor on which there grew a purple-flowered vine. Down another flight of stairs were more tables and a little building which had a counter in it. There were what looked like a tray of sandwiches on the counter and an array of bottles behind it.

As I stood hesitating, a friendly middle-aged Greek appeared behind the counter from a back room. He beckoned and said, "Buy here. Take to table." I had eaten the last remnants of my lunch supplies up on the site and was still hungry, so I thanked him in Greek and managed to order a soft drink and a sandwich without too many grammatical errors. Once the man found I spoke a little Greek he patiently let me practice it on him, correcting my pronunciation occasionally. Some Greeks insist on practicing their English on you, and a few are impatient with foreigners' stumbling Greek; but a great many Greeks have the endearing habit of encouraging you in your efforts to speak their language and cheerfully correcting your mistakes.

The prices were high but not outrageous, and the place was so beautiful and the man so friendly I didn't mind paying more than I would have in town. I found a table at the edge of the terrace under the arbor and found I had a magnificent view across the valley, framed in purple flowers. A little stream of water trickled down the hill at the edge of the terrace, making a musical sound in my ears as I munched my sandwich and drank my pop—a bottled lemon soda, tart and refreshing.

It had struck me while I talked to the man at the counter that there was a mystery about how I had talked to the priestess and to Apollo. They hadn't spoken English—that was ridiculous—but I had understood every word and had not had to fumble for words in my reply. I tried to remember words I had said or which had been said to me, but it was hard; I remembered the sense of what had been said, as if it had been said in English. What had Apollo kept calling me? I remembered it as "girl," but how had it sounded? *Koré*, I was sure he had said—the ancient Greek word for "girl," not any of the modern Greek equivalents. It seemed as if along with the change in my clothes and water bottle, something—or someone—had given me the ability to speak and understand ancient, or more likely archaic, Greek while I was on the other side of the mists.

I had just reached this point in my ponderings when a very good-looking young man with a mop of blond hair and a spectacular tan sat down at a neighboring table and drummed his fingers impatiently as he waited for service.

"You have to go in the little room down there and bring your order to the table yourself," I told him, hoping he spoke English— I would have guessed that he was Scandinavian.

He gave a little bow and said in somewhat accented English, "You are very kind. I thank you for saving me from wasting my time waiting here." He went off to the counter leaving me wondering if my impression that he was rather pompous was due just to his somewhat stilted English.

When he returned, he bowed again; in fact, he almost clicked his heels, but that's difficult to do in Adidas. "You permit?" he said, and sat down at my table without waiting for me to answer. I soon found that his name was Kurt Braun, that he was German, and also that the pomposity was very real and not just an effect of his formal English. After a very sketchy interrogation to find out my name and nationality, Kurt Braun began talking about what seemed to be his favorite subject, himself. I was treated to a quick sketch of his academic career and his brilliant prospects, and then I was taken in hand and instructed on the proper opinion to hold on all matters about Delphi—according to that eminent expert Kurt Braun.

Since he had let slip that he was only a sophomore and since many of his deliverances were straight out of the standard guidebooks, I was not convinced. I had done a lot of preliminary reading for Delphi, and I knew that most of the guidebook platitudes were highly questionable according to the real scholars. The underground fumes were a myth; so probably was the idea that the Delphi prophetesses babbled unintelligible words which were "interpreted" by priests. But when I tried to challenge his dogmatic assertions, my arguments were ignored. If I cited an authority, there was some German authority who knew better. Since I had admitted to being only a freshman at college, and an early entrant from an accelerated high school program at that, I was in effect told to listen to my elders and betters. I was annoyed, but it had its funny side.

It soon developed that this display of erudition was supposed to impress me into accompanying Kurt to one of the local discos that night. My excuses were brushed aside; my work couldn't possibly be more important than abetting his amusements. I was about to resort to outright rudeness when I looked over Kurt's head and saw the young man who had accosted me the night before, his dark eyes amused. "Oh, Nikos, there you are," I said with a little more warmth than I had intended. "I think I'm ready to go now."

Nikos played it up beautifully. He nodded to Kurt in a friendly but dismissive fashion, took my daypack in one hand and my arm in the other, and had ushered me up the steps before Kurt could say a word. I looked back from the top of the steps to see Kurt on his feet beside the table, looking dumbfounded and beginning to grow angry as he stared after us.

# CHAPTER
# FIVE

As we walked down the road, Nikos turned to me with a conspiratorial grin, and suddenly we were laughing together. "The young German is not very quick," said Nikos. "I think he is astonished that you choose a non-Aryan companion when you could have one who is *echt deutsch*." His face sombered. "No, that is not fair; because he is a German does not mean he is Nazi." Then he grinned again. "But it did look as if he were trying to invade some territory when I rescued you."

I laughed. "I admit that you rescued me, but mainly from being bored to death," I said.

He shook his head, laughing. "Not just bored, I think. When he wouldn't listen to your ideas, I could almost see fire coming out of your eyes."

This meant that Nikos had been listening to us for at least a little while before I saw him at the door. I didn't much like the idea that he had been eavesdropping on us, and I was suddenly very conscious that his hand was still on my arm. "I'm not sure that Greek men are any better at listening to ideas when they come from a woman," I said challengingly.

He looked at me quizzically but with a smile in his eyes. "Ah, that depends on the man, I think," he said. "But anyway, a Greek would *pretend* to listen, especially if the woman were beautiful. Now I am very interested in *your* views. What do you think of my hometown?"

"I love it," I said, flattered just as he intended by the subtle implication that *I* was a beautiful woman—though I tried to feel proper feminist outrage that the alleged beauty was the reason my

views were worth listening to. "Are you really from Delphi itself?"
I asked.

He nodded. "Our family olive groves are down in the valley
there, but Delphi is our village," he said. "And I live mostly in
Athens now, but Delphi is my home."

"What do you do in Athens?" I asked, wondering if the answer
would give me a clue to his age.

"Study at the Polytechnic," he said, and then added with a grin,
"when it doesn't interfere with my social life."

"Your English is marvelous," I said. "I just hope my Greek will
be as good someday."

He grinned. "Then you must remember that when you speak *to*
me you say 'Niko,' not 'Nikos.' Do you know why?"

"Oh, of course, it's a vocative, isn't it?" I said. "I really do know
some grammar, but it's hard to remember grammar when you're
in a hurry."

"And you were in a hurry to get away from the talkative young
German," he said solemnly but with a glint of humor in his eyes.
"And now perhaps you are in a hurry to get away from the talkative
Greek."

"You're much better company, Niko," I said, and was rewarded
with a brilliant smile which made it hard to go on. "But I really
have to do some shopping and wash some things before dinner."

"Ah, shopping and washing, very proper occupations for a woman,"
he said with a straight face, but I was already beginning to learn
when he was teasing and didn't rise to the bait. He went on. "And
your studies occupy your evenings as I heard you tell the young
German. But you said 'before dinner,' so you do take time to eat.
*Leepon*—that means 'therefore' and is a very useful Greek word—
*leepon*, you will be my guest, please, for dinner to welcome you to
Delphi on behalf of my village. You must say '*endaxi*,' which means
'okay.' "

"Okay," I said. "I mean, *endaxi*. And *efkaristo pollee, O Niko*."

"You say 'thank you' very nicely," he told me gravely. "But I
cannot say it back because I do not yet know your name."

"I'm sorry, I should have told you before," I said, though I'm
not sure when I would have had time. "My name is Alice, Alice

Grant. You know I'm an American, I guess. I'm from Washington—the state, not the city. It's on the West Coast."

He nodded. "I have a cousin in Seattle," he told me. We chatted amicably about Seattle until he dropped me at my hotel with a handshake that was only a little warmer and more lingering than was called for.

I sat on the bed later that evening, shopping and washing done, scribbling some postcards. It had been a fantastic day in every sense of the word, and I wished there were someone I could discuss it all with. It was certainly not a day I could write anyone about. I grinned as I imagined a letter to my father: "I've met three young men, each as handsome as a Greek god. In fact, one of them *is*."

My life was certainly getting complicated, in more ways than one. But the very fact that interesting things were happening to me in the here and now made me all the more sure that my experiences in the past were not some kind of wish-fulfilling delusion. Anyway, there had been so much terror as well as so much wonder in my experience with Apollo and the Pythia that it was hard to think of the events which had taken place as any kind of wish fulfillment.

The experience just ahead of me had its terrors too. I had skipped a grade early in grammar school, and from then on I was younger and smaller than my classmates. I had compensated by working even harder at my studies, and as a result, I had never had much social life. I had a few close friendships with other girls and a few strictly platonic friendships with boys; but most of my socializing had been with groups of people, and the few times I'd been out alone with a boy I'd been unsure of myself and uncomfortable. It hadn't helped that my own mother had died when I was ten and that my father had remarried, a younger woman with whom I didn't get along very well.

Greek men, with their enthusiastic pursuit of any passable-looking foreign girl, had been a great boost to my ego, but I soon found that they wanted to score in more than one sense; a foreign girlfriend was much more a trophy than a person. Nikos *seemed* different, but maybe he was just more dangerous because he had a sense of humor and used a little imagination in his approach rather than a hard sell. The fluttering in my stomach as I put on the only good dress I had brought and brushed out my hair was as much from fear as from excitement.

I was sitting on my little balcony, pretending to read a guide-book, when Nikos appeared, not really late by Greek standards, and called up to me. I tried to walk down the stairs at less than my usual headlong pace and found Nikos in the tiny lobby in voluble conversation with Kyria Amalia. Of course, I realized Nikos, who had grown up in Delphi, would probably know other permanent residents such as Kyria Amalia; it was a small town after all. They might even be related.

Kyria Amalia came over to me, exclaiming about how nice I looked "in a proper dress" and maneuvered me over to a little mirror in the lobby, just barely out of earshot from where Nikos lounged near the door. "With Kyrios Petrides I don't worry about you like I would with some boys," she murmured as she fussed with my hair. It took me a minute to realize that "Kyrios Petrides" was Nikos. "But a man is a man," she went on, "so to make sure, I told him how young you are; I know from your passport. So it will be all right. He is *evgenikos*—what do you say? A gentleman." And she bustled off, very pleased with herself.

I was so mortified that I could hardly say a word to Nikos as we walked down the street to the restaurant he had chosen. I was not planning to let Nikos add me to what I was sure was a long line of conquests, but I was sure that he was *evgenikos* enough to take no for an answer without Kyria Amalia's meddling. Nikos didn't seem to notice and kept up a cheerful, inconsequential chatter while we went down some steps to a restaurant perched on the side of the hill overlooking the valley.

When we were seated, though, he looked at me and was silent for a moment. Then he said gently, "Amalia Nomikou means well, you know, but she is a silly old woman. She does not have to tell me your age to protect you from me. With me you do not need protection. But I am glad she told me because it helps me to know you a little more. You are more mature than many girls I have met; at your age this is all the more remarkable." He grinned. "I am twenty-three," he said. "Do you think for my age I am not very mature?"

I laughed, and he laughed back at me, and suddenly my feeling of awkwardness was gone. "There's a line in . . . a book I like," I told him, "that goes something like 'The stupidest children are the most childish and the stupidest grown-ups are the most grown-up.' I really don't think age is all that important to being mature."

Nikos nodded thoughtfully. "I think I agree with your book," he said. "Clever children are often not childish, and great men very often have something of the child in them. What is the name of this book?"

"It's a children's book," I told him, not embarrassed to say so, as I might have been a few minutes earlier, "called *The Silver Chair*. It's a fantasy—a sort of fairy tale, but lots of grown-ups like it."

Nikos nodded, "I, too, like some books for children, especially ones about our Greek mythology. When they try to retell the myths for adults, they spoil them somehow. In some ways I think people in the old times were more like children than people now—not stupid children but clever children. Those who retell the myths for clever children today sometimes hit the right note. *The Silver Chair*: that sounds like something out of our myths. Theseus, I think, when he went down to Hades, sat in a silver chair and could not get up again."

"This book isn't about Greek myths really," I told him, "but the man who wrote it knew a lot about mythology, and he used bits from lots of myths. Maybe the silver chair does come from the Theseus story because it is in an underworld and it does imprison the person in it." I looked around the restaurant, which was a charming place with outdoor tables on a terrace overlooking the valley. There was a songbird in a cage hanging from the awning over the tables, and a cheerful young boy was bustling around, cleaning tables and taking orders. I realized that I was enjoying myself very much.

We talked about books and mythology through a delicious meal. I had a glass of the unresinated local wine that Nikos was having with his meal and found it much easier to like than the resinated wine, retsina, which I was still trying to get used to. Nikos was pleased that I was trying to like typically Greek things such as retsina and, when we finished our meal, asked if I'd like to stroll up the street to a *kafeneion* and try Greek coffee. "Oh, I've had it and I like it, but it's too sweet for me. Could I have it with no sugar at all?" I said.

He made a face. "You may certainly have it that way if you like, but mostly we drink coffee *sketo*—without sugar—only for when we have a hangover. It is very bitter that way, you know."

"Yes, but that way it makes a contrast with those wonderful sweet pastries," I said.

He laughed. "Okay, you can also have one of those. I am glad to see that you like sweet things *too*."

I was a little abashed. "I did eat a lot at dinner, didn't I? Niko, that was a very expensive meal, and I notice that you had liver while I was having souvlakia. You're still a student yourself, and I don't want to . . ." I trailed off. Nikos was quite liberated for a Greek male, but I knew I could never get him to let me share the cost of a meal or buy him even a coffee.

Nikos laughed. "Don't worry," he said. "My pockets are not *quite* empty. When I am home, I am rich because I do not have to pay for meals and lodging, and because I help with the olives, I get a share of the money which they make. Most of that goes in the bank, and in Athens I try to live on my grant. For these researches of yours you have a grant perhaps?"

"No," I said, "my trip to Greece comes out of my college money that my grandmother put in the bank for me when I was little. I've added to it a little from baby-sitting and summer jobs—picking berries mostly. It took a lot of lugs of strawberries, raspberries, and blueberries to pay my way over here, but it was worth it."

"And your parents are not worried that you live in a strange country on your own?" persisted Nikos.

I hesitated. It wasn't his business—at least at this stage of our friendship—that Irene, my stepmother, was glad to have me halfway around the world instead of in "her" home and that Dad seemed just as glad to have me stay away for the summer instead of living at home and bickering with Irene. This trip had been my declaration of independence from Dad as well as from Irene, and I was secretly a little dismayed at how easily he had let me go. But I could tell Nikos the more impersonal facts about my coming to Greece.

"Well, I didn't start off on my own," I told him. "I came over with a study tour from the university; they have a regular program in Greece for the whole spring quarter. When the program ended, the two faculty members stayed on—one to run a summer program and one to do some research on her own. I have to do a research project myself this summer. It's one of the requirements for the program that let me graduate from high school early and enter the university. I suppose I could have done it at home, but I wanted to stay over here and study one place in Greece in depth. We did so much moving around on the tour that I never felt that I got to really know any place well. So I stayed on in the student hostel in Athens with the faculty members after the spring group had left and did a lot of reading in the libraries there. I got interested in Delphi and decided to do the actual writing on the project while I lived here and soaked up some atmosphere. My adviser, Professor Pennyquick, allowed me to do it; he encourages students to get off on their own and really experience Greece. But he's in Athens most of the time if I need help."

"I am glad you told me this," said Nikos seriously, "because the first thing my mother said when I told her about you was 'Why does her family let her live here all alone in a hotel?' We are old-fashioned here, you understand, especially in the villages. If one of our girls went to America and lived alone in a hotel, everyone here would think bad things about her."

"Probably some of the old biddies at home think bad things about *me*," I said with a laugh I tried to make careless. Probably Irene does too, I added to myself. I was considerably shaken up by the fact that Nikos had discussed me with his mother; it meant that he didn't regard me just as a summer pickup. I was glad of that, but I wasn't sure that I really wanted him to be as serious about me as he now seemed to be.

Nikos seemed to realize that he had let slip more than he intended; he seemed to make an effort to get away from personal topics. "Yes, we also have old ladies who like to gossip, but it is more than that: The villages are many years behind the times. There are many superstitions, many strange beliefs. Delphi is not a typical village because of all the visitors, but even here there are superstitions. Some of the shepherds claim to have seen the nymphs dancing, up on the slopes of Parnassos."

Suddenly I realized that I had a chance to discuss, however

obliquely, some of the things that had been going around in my head since that morning. "Niko," I said, "do you think there's any truth to the old stories about nymphs and gods? Like Apollo, for example?"

From the tone of his voice when he had spoken of village superstitions I half expected him to scoff, but his tone was far from scornful as he said, "The gods—that is a puzzle. Our Greek gods, you know, were very human, very much like men and women in their loves and hates, their affairs and quarrels. Some people now say that the gods were visitors from space; but the old stories say that they could have children by ordinary humans, and I do not think that an alien race could do that. Perhaps, after all, they were humans who discovered some source of power that has been lost, as in the tales they tell of the wise men of India. But that there was some reality beyond the tales, something besides just imagination—yes, this I believe. Yet what it was I cannot say."

I was tempted to confide in him, to pour out the story of what had happened to me that morning. But our relationship was still too fragile. He did not know me well enough to believe a story so fantastic just on my word; I did not know him well enough to be sure that he would not think me crazy or a liar. "What about your local god, Apollo?" I asked, trying to keep my tone light.

His smile flashed briefly; then he was serious again. "We have two 'local gods' at Delphi, you know," he said. "The shrine and the Temple were Apollo's, but the hills and the caves belonged to Dionysos. And in the winter months Delphi belonged to Dionysos entirely. And to tell you the truth, I think I like Dionysos the better of the two. Oh, I admire the clarity and beauty associated with Apollo, just as I admire the brilliance and warmth of the sun. But the sun can be merciless, the sun can kill. Here in the 'lands of the sun' the sun is not entirely a friend; it can dry and burn the crops, kill men with thirst or sunstroke. We run from the sun to the kindly shade. And there is very little mercy or laughter or love in the cult of Apollo. He is a god of light, a god of beauty. But he is also a god who cut down men with his merciless arrows when he was offended. Apollo is a killer."

*     *     *

As I lay in my bed at the end of that eventful day, two faces danced in my brain: the dark face of Nikos; the golden face of Apollo. And two voices echoed in my dreams: the calm, beautiful voice of the god and the quiet but impassioned voice of Nikos. One voice said, "The Path will open for you again," and the other said, "Apollo is a killer."

# CHAPTER SIX

The next morning I rushed out to the site as soon as I could get away from Kyria Amalia and her probing questions about my dinner with Nikos. This time there was no conveniently unguarded gate, and I had to wait with the other early comers until the gate opened officially at nine o'clock. It was the first time I used my pass, and it was carefully scrutinized by both guards on duty at the gate with much discussion between them and many comparisons of the photograph on the pass with my face. Eventually they let me in; but by that time the other early comers had straggled up the path ahead of me, and there was no chance of reaching the Rock alone. And all that morning I seemed to be constantly encountering curious or suspicious glances from guards or from some of the tourists who had seen them discussing my pass.

At lunchtime I gave up and left the site to have my lunch at the little café on the hillside near the Castalian Spring. I felt guilty at just buying a bottle of pop and eating my lunch at one of the tables, so I finished off my lunch by buying ice cream, only to find that it was one of the most overpriced things on the menu.

It was delicious, though, and as I ate it slowly, I tried to make plans. I had made too much of a stir today to have much chance at quietly hiding out on the site until the gates closed. Furthermore, I wasn't sure that I could get out once the site was locked up, and I could imagine Kyria Amalia's comments if I stayed out all night. The story would probably get right back to Nikos, too, and might give him second thoughts about my youth and innocence.

Despondently I decided to abandon for today any attempt to get to the Rock alone and unobserved. I spent the afternoon in and around the museum, and when it closed for the day, I went back to my room for a siesta. I couldn't expect Nikos to buy me a dinner every day, but I wouldn't mind just a walk or a coffee with him— if he should ask me. I drifted into pleasant daydreams, and by the time I fell asleep I was sure he *would* ask me.

I woke up late in the evening feeling thickheaded and grumpy. There was no sign of Nikos and no message from him in my box at the desk in the lobby. I slouched off to look for dinner, ducking quickly out the door when I saw Kyria Amalia coming down the stairs. I was in no mood for any further interrogations about Nikos.

I had a not very tasty meal of moussaka and salad at a little café near the Delphi youth hostel. The moussaka was the kind with lots of potatoes and very little meat, and as I munched my way through the stodgy food, my mood of disgruntlement gradually deepened. I eventually convinced myself that Nikos *had* been put off by what Kyria Amalia had told him about my age and that he had taken me out for that evening only out of politeness. I'd probably never see him again.

I heard a slight cough and looked up to see the young German, Kurt Braun, looking very woebegone. "You are alone?" he asked hesitantly. When I nodded, he asked, "Perhaps you would like some coffee?"

I decided to be nice to him and said yes. After all, Nikos wasn't the only handsome young man in Delphi, and if he didn't want to buy me a coffee, others evidently did. When Kurt wasn't being pompous, he was really rather attractive, I told myself. If Kurt behaved himself, then if Nikos showed up later, it might be he who got the brush-off this time.

Once Kurt had returned with two Nescafés, he was on his best behavior, asking me how I'd spent the day and actually listening to my answers. We talked a little about the museum. I could see that he wanted to lay down the law again when I said I didn't like the statue of Antinoüs, who had been the boyfriend of a Roman emperor. But he didn't dogmatize *too* much about how, according to the German experts, it was a great work of art.

When our talk turned to the site, I mentioned casually how much I had enjoyed getting in ahead of the crowd my first day and how hard it was to appreciate the ruins when they were so crowded with tourists. He lowered his voice conspiratorially and glanced around to see if we were overheard as he said, "It is not hard to slip into the site at night. Some of my friends and I have done it already. Would you like me to show you how to do it? The ruins will be beautiful by moonlight."

It seemed a wonderful chance to get to the Rock alone, and if Nikos didn't like my going off with Kurt, he should have been here himself. I agreed enthusiastically, not realizing that Kurt Braun might get the wrong impression about my reasons.

He led me up the village streets, then, when these petered out, up a gravel road to a gate in a wire fence. "There is a house in there. I think perhaps it belongs to the curator of the site," he said. "At any rate, whoever lives there has an automobile, and sometimes this gate is unlocked when the automobile is out."

This time, though, the gate was locked. Kurt shrugged and said, "We must follow the fence, then, to a place higher up the hill where there are trees overhanging the fence." After a considerable scramble uphill we finally found the place he meant, where a climbable tree had a large branch that drooped over the fence. I followed him out on the limb and let him help me down. It wouldn't be hard to get back up on the branch with Kurt to boost me, but I wanted to lose him and head for the Rock.

"If we get separated, how do I get back over the fence?" I asked in a voice I tried to make casual.

"Oh, we won't get separated," said Kurt in a voice that was full of all his old arrogance. "And why worry about getting back? We should enjoy the moonlight while we can." His arm slipped around my waist, making it quite clear how *he* intended to enjoy the moonlight. I knew that I was being unreasonable, but my realization that I had probably led him on by being so eager for this late-night expedition alone with him only increased my fury. Men! When they didn't ignore you, they took you for granted; they never asked what *you* wanted.

"Let go," I said, but he only held me tighter. I twisted to one side, stamped on his foot, and drove an elbow into his midriff. He gasped, lost his footing on the sloping ground, and fell into a bush. A prickly bush, to judge from his howls. Serves him right, I thought vindictively, and slipped into the shadows among the trees. My explorations the day before paid off now; it was easy enough even in the moonlight to find one of the paths that led toward the center of the site. But as I got closer to the main ruins, the moon went behind a cloud, and I had to creep ahead cautiously to keep from taking a nasty tumble on the uneven, rock-strewn ground.

As I got closer to the dark bulk that must be one of the bigger ruins, it seemed to get darker yet. I began to be less sure of just where I was in the ruins. Did this path come out above the Rock or below it? How could it be this dark on a night that had been clear only a little while ago? I began to panic a little. Did the guards patrol the site at night? Surely I heard a footstep ahead of me. A guard or an angry Kurt Braun looking for me?

Then I felt a familiar tingle in my body. I was near the Rock or at least somewhere on the—what had Apollo called it?—Line of Power. I walked forward cautiously until the tingling sensation increased, then decreased. I backed up until the sensation was at its greatest, then hesitated. Should I go uphill or down? The tingle was very strong. I was sure that the Path, as the god had called it, was open. But if I went away from the Rock instead of toward it, what would happen?

It was dark around me, unnaturally dark, and I was completely disoriented now. All I could do was make a blind choice. Remembering that I had walked uphill on my first journey through the Path, I turned and began to walk. I felt the ground rise under my feet, and this gave me some confidence, even through the darkness. Although there was no sign of the mist that had surrounded me on the other occasion, I did not feel that I was walking in the everyday world.

There was no sign of the Rock, either, but eventually I saw a light ahead of me—not the glare of an electric light or the strange golden glow I had seen coming from Apollo's body in the shadow of the serpent, but a red dancing light that could come only from a fire. At first I wondered if I could have blundered onto a group of guards burning rubbish, but then I heard voices—women's voices and lots of them.

There was darkness behind me; I couldn't go back; I had to face whatever awaited me in the fitful red glow of that fire. As I came closer, I saw that beside the fire some of the women were holding torches. In the flickering light of the fire and the torches I could see that there were only women in the group and that they were not in any kind of modern clothing but in the flowing robes of the classical age. I looked down at my own clothing and saw that I was now dressed the same way.

As I came to the edge of the group of women, the tingle in my body lessened but did not entirely disappear. A woman detached herself from the group and came and took me by the hands in a gesture that seemed warm and spontaneous but also held a hint of some ceremony of welcome. "Welcome, Sister," she said simply. "It will not be long now. *He* will soon be here." The tone of her voice told me it was no ordinary "he" she was speaking of. Could it be Apollo they were expecting? But this all-female gathering in darkness was like no worship of Apollo I had ever heard of.

Looking around me, I saw that some of the women wore ceremonial garb, some sort of shawl or short cloak of a soft dark material, dappled in white. A few of them also held long staffs in their hands, each with a bulbous protuberance at the top. I drifted closer to one of the women and saw that her cloak or shawl was hide or fur and the protuberance at the top of her staff was a large pine cone. Something tickled at my memory. I could see a crown of leaves on her head, and a moment later one of the other women pressed a similar crown onto my hair. I could feel the atmosphere of tense expectancy around me, increasing and increasing until it was like a physical pressure.

Suddenly there was a piercing cry, the *wildest* sound I have ever heard. Every eye turned in the direction from which the call had come. Standing on a little hillock above us was a figure that shone with the same golden glow I had seen coming from Apollo's skin as he fought the Pythia. The figure was male and young, but it was not the figure of Apollo!

In some ways this young man—or god—could hardly have been different from Apollo. His hair was a crisp black, and its curls were as casually windswept as the curls of Apollo's golden head had been disciplined. His eyes were blue like Apollo's, but a deeper blue than Apollo's had been, and whereas Apollo's eyes had radiated an arrogant authority, this young man's were full of what I could only call mischief—something wild and impudent and reckless. This face did not have the cold beauty of Apollo's, though it was beautiful enough with a beauty that had a touch of the feminine and a touch of the oriental. In place of Apollo's cold smile this young man had a grin that reminded me fleetingly of Nikos; he looked as if he were enjoying himself and wanted you to enjoy yourself. His figure was motionless, but you felt that it might explode into violent motion any second; he seemed to vibrate with life. His head was wreathed with the same leaves as those the woman wore, and he wore one of the dappled skins draped around his tunic.

The women greeted him with ecstatic cries of *"Io, Io Bromio!"* That was one of his names, but I knew another. "Dionysos," I gasped. Across the crowd of ecstatic women his eyes met mine, and he gave me a slow smile full of intimacy; we might have been old friends—or lovers. When his eyes left me, I was shaken; I felt that in comparison to that look, no other man, not even Nikos, had ever *really* looked at me, *really* seen me.

Dionysos gave that piercing cry again and beckoned with a sweeping motion of his left hand. "To the hills!" he cried. He leaped up the hill, agile and light-footed as a wild goat, and we streamed after him. I was filled with a wild exultation. Was this what it felt like to be drunk? But surely drunkenness robbed you of coordination, and I had never felt so strong and agile in my life. Near me a stout little woman with a crown of leaves in her gray hair was leaping from rock to rock, holding up her long skirt in both hands. I found myself laughing. My laughter was echoed by others around me. Two younger women helped the gray-haired woman to kilt up her skirt by pulling it up through the cord around her waist and letting it blouse over. The rest of us did the same, and we were off again after the hallooing god.

The remainder of that night remains in my memory only in flashes: running wild and free along the slopes of Parnassos, then, later, sprawling on the grass, laughing until we were weak. I remember sitting quietly, listening to the untrained but beautiful voice of one of the women as she sang old songs of love and war. Somewhere we found a little herd of deer, and at the call of Dionysos they came and nuzzled us. The fawns gamboled and played with us as if we, too, were fawns. One full-breasted woman took the smallest fawn in her arms and nursed it as if it were her baby.

Something soft brushed my bared leg, and I looked down without surprise to see a spotted leopard rubbing itself against me as if it were a cat. Another leopard was playing among the deer; they showed no fear of it, and it did nothing to harm them.

As the first pale light of dawn began to touch the eastern hills, the women broke into small groups or couples talking earnestly to one another. I wish I could remember these conversations; it seemed to me that I had never before talked so deeply or so honestly to any woman, not to my mother, not to my best friends. Then—I don't know how long after—I found myself sitting in the strengthening light of dawn, sitting on a log in a little grassy glade. Beside me was Dionysos, his dark blue eyes probing into mine with disturbing intensity.

# CHAPTER SEVEN

"So you're the girl 'Pollo called from beyond the Divide," Dionysos said, as if he were continuing a conversation we had started long ago. "And what do you think of it all?" He grinned at me, reminding me of Nikos. I realized that I felt as much at ease with him as I did with Nikos—more at ease, for I felt that there was no possibility of misunderstanding between Dionysos and me.

"It's like *A Midsummer Night's Dream*," I said, thinking mostly of that night's experience. "Oh, but you wouldn't know about that, unless—"

He shook his head. "I don't have Apollo's power to see the future, and I won't rummage through your mind without permission. But if you'd concentrate on your memories of whatever it was you were talking about . . ." He paused, while I tried to concentrate on memories of a performance of the play I had seen not long ago. He gave a little crow of laughter and said, "How marvelous! *Actors* you call them, and a *theater*. And the words they spoke are poetry, but like ordinary speech too. There are possibilities in that, great possibilities. . . ." I realized with a little thrill of strangeness that he had *seen* those things as I had remembered them.

"But all that—acting, the theater—started from ceremonies which were held to honor you," I said.

He grinned at me. "Will start, my dear, will start. Let me dip into your mind again. . . . I see: theaters, *my* theaters not only here but in Athens and other places. Wonderful, I'll like that. A much more sensible way to honor *me* than hymns and sacrifices. There's nothing so boring as being worshiped."

I stared at him. "But if you feel that way . . ." I began.

He chuckled. "*I* feel that way," he said, "but that's not to say that the other Olympians do. It's an insidious thing, being worshiped. I joke about it, but I've felt the temptation. I tell myself I let myself be worshiped so I can accomplish what I'm trying to accomplish with the women, but the craving to be worshiped can grow. I've seen it with the others."

"What *are* you trying to accomplish with these women?" I asked.

He looked at me for a long moment, then spoke slowly. "It's not something I speak of to many. My mother was a mortal woman. She was injured terribly by her contact with the Olympians. I've sworn to make that injury up to other women as best I can. I can't change the way women are treated in this time and place as much as I'd like, but I can give them freedom for a little while, freedom and sharing together and the strength that comes from those things."

"That's wonderful," I said. "I was part of it tonight, and I know what you mean about the sharing and the freedom."

His face was somber. "Not always so wonderful," he said. "When you set free the emotions of a woman who has been hurt and oppressed, they can run free in some strange ways. Tonight you saw the *thiasos*—the women who follow me—playing with the animals, but there have been times when the *thiasos* have killed animals, even torn them to pieces. It sickened me, but perhaps it was better that their rage and frustration be released that way than in other ways. Better, perhaps, a poor animal than a husband or child."

I shuddered. "There are stories told in my time," I said, "of men who tried to stop your worshipers—"

He nodded, his face grim. "Those who come among my women with hate and murder in their hearts can provoke a terrible response. I cannot always prevent these things from happening; once I have looked into the minds of the intruders, I do not always want to."

I looked into the face of the god and was afraid for the first time. Here was no god of mercy and forgiveness but a being of immense powers, as wild and dangerous as one of his leopards. I, too, was an intruder in his rites; what would happen to me if I offended him?

Dionysos looked into my eyes and smiled. "Have no fear," he said softly. "No woman—and no man of goodwill—has anything to fear from me. I know how easily an Olympian can harm a mortal, even without intending to. It was so when Zeus blasted my mother, though others were not guiltless in that affair." There was a grim expression about his mouth, and I would not have liked to have been those "others" even if they were gods. Then his face grew sad. "Some say I have driven women mad," he said, "my aunts, among others. But what I did was touch them with my power as I touched you tonight, and their hates and fears overwhelmed their minds." He smiled a wry grin and said, "Some say all who follow my call are mad. Do you feel mad? For you are a maenad now, a wild bacchante."

I smiled back at him, my fears gone. "I suspect it's a lot like being what they call in my time an uppity woman, and I've always been that a bit. A young man I pushed into a thorny bush tonight would certainly say so."

Dionysos grinned. "I suspect he deserved it," he said. "A man who tries to force a woman so she must use force in return is twice a fool, for even if he gains what he seeks, he loses forever the gift in freedom he might have had from her. But you remind me that you have come a long journey and perhaps have been out of your own time long enough. Even the wisest of us knows too little of these matters. Must you return to the *place* you came from?"

I thought of the difficulty of getting out of the site, the possibility of running into an angry Kurt or being caught by the guards. "No," I said. "In fact, I'd rather not."

He laughed. "The young man in the thornbush? You could face him down; you are a maenad now. But it is just as well. There is something I would like to show you. Come."

We rose to our feet, and he led the way through the bushes at the side of the little grove, up a little hill and among the first straggling houses of a village. A short walk led us to a big central area, a grassy field surrounded by small houses. In the center of the field were most of the women who had been my companions on this night of adventure, some asleep, some merely sprawled on the ground in exhaustion. Little knots of men stood on the outskirts of the field, muttering to one another. There was an angry note in their voices, and I felt a stab of apprehension for the women, defenseless in their exhaustion. I turned to Dionysos.

"No need for me," he murmured. "Watch." I became aware that one by one the doors of the houses were opening, and the women of the village were coming out onto the dirt lanes that served as streets. They walked quietly up to the group of women and then turned and faced the men. Before long there was a circle of village women surrounding the bacchantes, facing away from them and confronting their husbands, fathers, and brothers. The angry note in the men's voices died out into uncertainty.

There was a noise from one of the larger "streets," and a little group of men who looked as if they had walked long and far came up the street. One of them pointed at the bacchantes with an angry cry, and they surged forward. But now the village men stepped in their path, and there was a long discussion, which led to the group of angry travelers' turning away, frustrated. I did not need any explanation; what had happened was clear. The village women had protected the bacchantes from the wrath of their own men, and those men in turn had protected their own women and the bacchantes from men outside the village. Women had protected women; neighbors had protected neighbors. Protection did not mean approval, I was sure, but it was a start.

In my ears I heard the voice of Dionysos, but it seemed to come from above me and far away. "Now my blessings on this village of Amphissa, so far as my blessings will reach. Let its women and men be healthy and happy; let its fields flourish. And—let its olives be the best in all the world!" As the voice spoke, the scene before my eyes seemed to freeze and fade, as if it were an old picture of times gone by. I blinked, and before my eyes the scene changed. I was standing in a paved square, with a fountain in the center and with tables and chairs set in the paved area around the fountain. On the street around the square, taxis and cars were parked. Children were running and playing around the square, and almost every chair at every table was occupied by one of a cheerful family group, talking and laughing. I was standing behind a little kiosk, but when I moved out of its shadow, no one seemed startled or surprised. I was back in my own time.

There was a bus parked at the edge of the square with "Delphi" written in Greek letters on its front, and I started to walk over to it, but I could see that it was locked up and dark; probably the last bus had gone, and this bus wouldn't return to Delphi until the morning. Then I heard a familiar voice calling me; I turned to find Nikos beaming at me.

"Alice!" he said, and I noticed how he hellenized my name so it was almost "Aleesah." He took my arm and gestured me to join him at a small table with a dark-haired man and a blond woman. "What brings you to Amphissa?" he asked. "Did you get my flowers?"

"Oh, I heard that the olives here are very good," I said, feeling very happy for some reason. "What flowers?" I added.

He made a clicking sound with his tongue. "Amalia Nomikou promised me she would give them to you with my apologies. I had to drive around the countryside on family business," he said. "How fortunate that we should meet in Amphissa."

"Perhaps it was arranged by Dionysos, whom you prefer to Apollo," I said.

I think he caught the note of seriousness in my voice, for he did not laugh but merely said quietly, "Perhaps." Then he turned to the man and woman and said in English, "This is Miss Alice Grant, who is in Delphi to study our history. Alice, this is my cousin Stavros Michaelides and his wife and partner, Berthe."

The man was a mustachioed Greek of middle height, and his wife had a round face with a dark tan and deep wrinkles at the corners of her eyes; I could picture her working outdoors day after day under a blazing sun. She said in good English but with a definite Germanic accent, "Take warning from me, Fräulein: Years ago I was a young foreign student. I sat down at a café table with a handsome young Greek, and now, ten years after, I am still sitting here."

Stavros Michaelides laughed and said in a deep voice, "And a good thing for me you did come to Amphissa, Berthe. I assure you, young lady, that she does not spend all of her time sitting here; it is her hard work that has made our land flourish."

"No," said Berthe Michaelides judiciously. "Many Greek women work much harder than I do. What they do not have is the knack of making their husbands work just as hard."

I thought that the laugh Stavros gave in response to this was a little forced, and Nikos tactfully directed the talk into other channels by repeating my remark about the olives of Amphissa. We spent a pleasant hour in general conversation while the light gradually faded and the square emptied of children. Berthe sighed. "Your mother will need help getting the boys to bed," she said to Stavros. To me she said, "I like my neighbors, but I enjoyed talking to a woman who is not Greek. Don't try to become Greek, Alice. It doesn't work unless you were born to it." With this enigmatic remark she hustled her husband off, and Nikos led me to a dusty but well-kept Datsun truck and we set off for Delphi.

He was silent for a while, and then he said quietly, "I don't hold up Stavros and Berthe as ideal; she is too bossy and he is too lazy. But I like it that in their work they are really partners. The land was from his family, some of the money for improvements was from hers, and they both worked hard. Now they are beginning to have success. Stavros wants to relax, she does not; sometimes they quarrel. But they do show, I think, that a foreign woman who marries a Greek need not fall into the pattern of the Greek wife. This, I think, is what Berthe meant when she said it does not work to become Greek."

Perhaps she meant that, I thought, and perhaps she meant, or half meant, that leaving her own country and language and culture was a decision she had regretted. But of course, she had an especially hard row to hoe in more senses than one as the wife of a farmer in a small village.

"What are you studying at the Polytechnic, Niko?" I asked.

"When I am graduated, I will be what you call a civic—no, civil—engineer," he said. "There is much work to do in our country improving roads, water supplies, communications. The government is trying to do something for the people in the villages, but it will take a long time—there is so much to do." He paused. "The work I will do is very much needed," he said quietly, "but it is not well paid, and I will spend much time in remote areas."

"Thank you for telling me, Niko," I said. We rode in silence awhile, both of us busy with our own thoughts. When we got to my hotel, I was just as glad that the traffic behind us and the strollers on the sidewalk discouraged much in the way of goodnights. Too much had happened today already. But I did want to be sure this time. "When will I see you again?" I asked directly.

He smiled warmly and took me by the hands. "It couldn't be too soon for me, but there are things the family counts on me for. Would you have dinner with me again on Saturday?"

"I'll be looking forward to it," I said. "Thank you for the ride, Niko. Until Saturday then." I slipped out of the car and into the hotel. Tired as I was, I knocked at Kyria Amalia's door and put up with her apologies and questions in order to get the flowers which Nikos had left for me. I put them on the table by the window, where I would see them in the morning, and went to bed to dream some very mixed-up dreams.

# CHAPTER EIGHT

Not surprisingly, I slept until noon the next day and awoke in no mood to face any of my problems. For the first time since I had come to Delphi I felt shut in by the mountains. I made a sketchy wash since the water was hot at Kyria Amalia's hotel for only a few hours in the morning and evening. I breakfasted on stale bread from yesterday morning and a warmish can of fruit juice, then walked out to the bus stop on the upper street, where the local buses stopped.

The first bus said "Itea," and I remembered that this was a seacoast town—the old port at which pilgrims had landed for Delphi. Suddenly the thought of immersing myself in cool seawater was irresistibly attractive. My swimsuit was at the hotel, but I had shorts and a sun halter in my daypack. Seawater wouldn't really do them much good, but they'd do to swim in and were getting pretty ragged anyway. I hopped aboard the bus with a feeling of going on vacation. My slight feeling of guilt about my much neglected research project only gave an edge to my get-away-from-it-all mood.

There were some spectacular views on the way down the mountain to the sea, but it was interesting inside the bus too. Like a lot of local buses in Greece, this one had a combination radio-cassette player on the dashboard near the driver. As soon as we got going, the driver pushed in a cassette and the bus was filled with Greek music. To enjoy Greece to the full, you have to learn to like Greek music as well as Greek food and wine, and I felt I was making progress on that. Sometimes I still got tired of the rather wailing love songs sung by nasal male singers, but I was beginning to recognize some of the singers and composers and to have my favorites. The music playing in the bus now was composed by Mikis Theodorakis, one of my favorites. I even knew the Greek words to one of the songs and sang them softly to myself.

I looked up to see the conductor, who had been working his way up the aisle, laughing and talking with the local people who made up most of the busload. He grinned at me and said, "You like the Greek music?"

"M'arehsee polee O Mikis Theodorakis," I said, showing off a bit. He laughed delightedly and exclaimed at my knowledge of Greek and Greek music. This led up to an invitation to go to the disco that night, as I might have expected. "My boyfriend wouldn't like that," I said. He asked if the boyfriend was Greek, and when I said yes, he gave up gracefully. I wasn't really sure that I could call Nikos a boyfriend or that he would really mind my going to the disco with someone else, but I had certainly found a good way to refuse unwanted offers politely. In fact, the whole incident left me feeling rather pleased with myself.

At first we seemed to be headed directly down to the sea after a brief stop at a tiny village near Delphi. Then we swung off in a direction parallel to the shore and, after a long drive through olive groves, pulled up in the little plaza in Amphissa where I had met Nikos the night before. The bus stopped, and the fare collector and driver got out and lit cigarettes; evidently the bus stopped here for a while.

It was interesting to see the little square again in daylight. I was tempted to stop here and explore Amphissa, but the thought of a cooling swim was even more attractive after almost a half hour on the bus. I did decide to get out of the bus and see as much as I could before it started up again. At a little kiosk in the square I saw a little pyramid of plastic jars, probably about a liter in size, without markings. I asked the old lady in the kiosk what was in them and she said, "Amphissa olives, very good," and pushed a jar toward me. Her pride in the local product was so obvious that I didn't have the heart to turn her down.

When I heard the bus motor start, I hastily pushed a 100-drachma note at her and pointed at the bus. She nodded, took the note, and didn't offer any change. Olives are awfully cheap in Greece, and 100 drachmas for a kilo seemed a little much, but of course, I was getting the plastic container free. I smiled, thanked her in Greek, and ran for the bus. She called something after me; I hoped I hadn't underpaid her or overpaid her. Greeks are quite honest, but when a foreigner overpays, they don't always make a great effort to straighten it out. Probably sometimes they let it go when they're underpaid because of language misunderstandings and figure that it all evens out.

The jar of olives didn't have any kind of handle and was really too big for my little daypack, so when the bus dropped me in Itea about fifteen minutes later, I had a rather awkward bundle to carry. Since I didn't know which way the beach might be, but I saw some tankers in the bay in one direction, I turned the other way. Soon I saw people lying on the sandy beach in swimsuits and outdoor showers at intervals for washing off the salt water after swimming. But there was no one in the water, and I wondered if the tankers or possibly sewage from the beachside hotels had polluted the water. I hiked on, hefting the olives and wishing I'd waited until the return trip to buy them.

Finally I got around a point of land, away from the tankers and hotels, and decided that I was so hot and tired I'd risk possible polluted water this close to town. The beach was deserted here, probably because it was rocky, and I saw a little tumbledown shack where I could probably change.

The shack was rather smelly, and the door didn't close all the way; but I was able to change into my shorts and halter in relative privacy. I picked my way down to the waterline through the stones and then realized I was hungry. I was low on lunch supplies again, but I did have bread, cheese, the olives, and water in my water bottle. I found a large flat rock to sit on, paddled my feet in the water, and had a light lunch. The olives were enormous and delicious, and soon I stopped regretting buying them.

When I finished, I tried to remember whether it was true that swimming right after a meal could give you cramps or whether it was one of those medical folktales with no substance. Then I looked far out to sea and saw a sleek form leap from the water. Could it possibly be a dolphin? I had been hoping to see dolphins ever since I came to Greece and had been unlucky every time. The closest I had got was a ferry trip on which some people claimed to have seen a dolphin from the deck while I was down below in the snack bar.

If that was a dolphin, it was awfully close to an inhabited area. Could it possibly be one of those superfriendly ones you hear about that was curious about people and not frightened of them? After all I had experienced in the past few days it might seem strange that I was thrilled at the thought of seeing a dolphin close too, but one of my childhood dreams had been to ride on a dolphin. I slipped into the water and swam for the place I had seen the shape.

The water was just right, not too warm and not too cool. After swimming out a little way, I dived and swam underwater a bit, wishing that I had brought my swimming goggles. I could see better than I expected, though, and I seemed to be able to swim farther than I thought I could before having to come up for breath. In fact, I felt a little frightened for a moment; surely I had been underwater much too long. But I was perfectly comfortable, and when at last my head broke water, I wasn't gasping for air but breathing normally.

I was tired, though, and I did a back float for a while, looking toward the shore. It looked deserted; funny that I couldn't see some of the taller hotels from here, even though there was that low promontory between where I was and the town. Then I heard a splash out at sea and quickly turned over and started swimming again.

There was that sleek shape, much closer now. That rounded dorsal fin had to belong to a dolphin! I glanced back at the shore to make sure that I wasn't getting dangerously far out and swam slowly toward the fin. I couldn't swim well and keep an eye on the fin, so I tried swimming for a while, then pausing to look. The second time I did this I saw a fin in a completely unexpected position. I looked over to where I had expected it to be and saw another two dolphins! Then a fourth sleek form broke the water. I must be in the middle of a school of them!

I had hardly got over the shock of this when I heard a creak and then a flapping sound. Perhaps there was a fishing boat here, and both the boat and the dolphins were pursuing a school of fish. I looked around for the boat, afraid that it might run me down before it saw me.

The boat was bearing down on me, but it was no fishing boat.

It was long and low with a narrow black hull, and it carried a big sail decorated with a design in a darker color than the brownish white of the sail. The sail was flapping so much now that I couldn't make out the design, but even so, the boat looked disturbingly unlike any modern boat. Surely I couldn't have gone back in time here in the ocean, so far from Delphi and its Path. But after all, Dionysos had sent me back to my own time at Amphissa, miles from Delphi; why couldn't the time journey in the other direction take place here, not all that much farther from Delphi than Amphissa itself?

The next minute any doubts were swept away. The sail bellied out in a gust of wind, showing that the design on it was an octopus with writhing tentacles, a design that might have come straight from an ancient Minoan vase. And the men peering over the side of the ship at me might have stepped out of a Minoan wall painting, with their ringleted long hair and bare torsos with a glint of jewelry at throat and wrist. This ship could only be from Crete!

"It's a girl, swimming," cried someone from the ship. "Heave to for a moment and throw her a rope."

"All right, all right," came a deeper voice. "But don't blame me if the mad creatures attack us again." A moment later I saw what the second voice had meant. The ship altered its course to lose way and pick me up, and immediately several dolphins hurled themselves at the side of the ship, battering at it as if to force it back on its course toward shore.

The rope they threw me had a lump of something soft on the end, which floated in the water. It was easy enough to swim over to it and get a good hold on it. As soon as I had it, the rope was rapidly hauled in, and I was grabbed by several strong arms and pulled over the low side of the ship. "Get her back on course for the shore," yelled one of the men as soon as I was aboard, "or they'll batter us to pieces."

I stood dripping onto what seemed to be a well-scrubbed deck and looked around me, very conscious that the two wisps of material that had replaced my shorts and halter covered very little. I would have liked just to stand and stare at this ship and its crew until I got my breath back, but a stocky man in a richly embroidered kilt came up to me and looked keenly into my face. He hesitated, then brought his hand to his forehead as if he were shading his eyes from the sun. "Bright Lady," he murmured.

"Are you mad, M'tano?" said a tall man in an equally elaborate kilt. "This is some fisher girl from a village on the shore."

The stocky man shook his head, his eyes fixed on me. "That may be, Akono," he said. "But I've sailed these seas for thirty years, and I've never seen dolphins act the way these have. Any girl I pick out of the sea from the midst of a bunch of god-possessed dolphins I'm going to presume is a goddess or one of the People of the Sea— no matter how human she looks—until I'm very sure that she's only what she seems. Anyway, a little courtesy won't hurt, even if she is a fisher girl." He turned back to me and said, "If those creatures are pets of yours, Lady, you can call them off. I'll beach my ship on the shore here; that is plainly what they want of me."

The tall man, Akono, scanned the shore with narrowed eyes. "You won't get the ship off again in a hurry if you run her ashore here," he said.

M'tano shrugged. "If whatever god wanted us to land here ever lets us go, the ship can be repaired," he said. "I'd have to draw her up for repairs somewhere whatever happened; she's barely sea-worthy now. And I'd rather wade ashore than swim ashore, espe-cially with the princess aboard. You'd best tell the ladies to brace themselves; we'll be running aground any minute." The taller man nodded and went off with a glum face. I saw that there was some sort of shelter astern, richly decorated and protected from the sun by shades or curtains.

M'tano was giving orders to his sailors, and I saw men standing by the ropes which led up to the big square of sail. When M'tano called out, "Now!" I expected to see the sail come down, but instead, it went *up*, drawn up to the upper spar like a curtain being raised. I could feel the ship lose way; then there was a crunching and rending sound, and the ship shuddered to a halt. There were cries and screams from the shelter aft; but the sailors were braced for the shock, and I had imitated them by finding a handhold and preparing myself for the impact.

M'tano bowed his head for a moment, and I saw tears in his eyes as he muttered to himself, "She was a good ship; may she sail again—though I doubt it." Then he turned to his men and began giving orders about what to unload first. The ship was listing a little, but it looked as if it were wedged in between large rocks that would hold it upright for a while.

Akono came bustling forward and said to M'tano, "My Lady sends her thanks, Captain, for bringing us safe ashore. If it's not safe for the ladies to stay aboard, they'll need some sort of shelter on the shore. Why don't you see if this girl speaks any civilized language and ask her about the nearest villages?"

I suppose it was then that I decided to say nothing for as long as I could. I certainly knew nothing about what villages might exist in this time; it didn't look as if there were even a fishing village where Itea would stand in my day. Amphissa might or might not exist now; I had a feeling that my adventure with Dionysos and his thiasos was somehow out of sequence with my first experience and this one. There was probably some sort of village at Delphi. Apollo had said that my later journeys in time would not take me back as far as my first one, and there had been a village near the site when I talked with the Pythia, I was sure; she had not seemed surprised when I said I came "from the village."

At any rate, M'tano seemed as reluctant to question me as I was to be questioned. "Let's get the ship unloaded before anything else," he said. "She won't last long on the rocks if these waves get any higher. If we lighten her, I think we can get her up on the beach and possibly make her seaworthy again." He looked out to sea, where a semicircle of rounded fins was visible and an occasional sleek shape could be seen above the waves. "Not that it looks as if that lot means to let us go, but our only road back to Kaphtu is the sea."

"Can we get to Pylos or at least get word there?" asked Akono. "They'd surely make every effort to get the princess safely there."

M'tano shrugged. "If I have any idea where we are, and I'm not sure that I do, Pylos of the sandy shores is across that gulf and clear across the Great Peninsula beyond, over some of the roughest country on the mainland. If I could patch up the ship and launch her, I could get her across the gulf and coast around the peninsula to Pylos. By land it would be a long, long journey. You'd have to go through Attica and past Corinth. In fact, I suspect that Corinth or Athens is the closest place that is what you'd call civilized."

Akono scowled. "I don't trust Corinth *or* Athens with a Kaphtui princess; she'd make too good a hostage. Athens, I suppose, if worse comes to worst; its people have some old ties with Pylos."

M'tano shook his head, his face grim. "What makes you think that whatever god or power brought us to this desolate shore will let us get anyplace else at all until we've served whatever purpose we've been brought here for?" he asked. And with a sudden chill I realized that those words applied to me every bit as much as to the passengers and crew of the wrecked ship.

# CHAPTER NINE

I watched in fascination as the crew prepared to beach the ship. First the spar with the sail on it was lowered down the mast. When I saw how much it obstructed the whole forward part of the ship, I realized why for the landing the sail had been raised up to the spar rather than the spar's being lowered, sail and all. Then the mast itself was unstepped and lowered onto a rest, so that it protruded from the bow of the ship like a bowsprit. The sailors now started to rotate the spar and sail so that it would lie parallel to the mast on the rest, but M'tano stopped them. "Unlace the sail and lay it on the beach; we'll stack cargo on it for the time being and make a tent of it later if necessary. Take it, spar and all, and unlace it on the shore."

The sail was quickly spread on the beach, and the crew began unloading cargo with practiced ease. Much of it was unrecognizable bales and bundles, but every so often I saw something I could identify: a bundle of long spears; some fire-blackened charcoal braziers; some amphorae that might have held wine or oil. A few men working under Akono's direction made a little shelter on the beach with lengths of cloth and reed matting and roughly furnished it with some of the softer bales. Then Akono went to the shelter on the stern of the ship and ushered out five women.

And what women! They were small and dark, with delicate features, but they moved with the grace of ballet dancers and the assurance of queens. They wore multi-flounced skirts that reached to their feet, but their short-sleeved jackets were open in front to reveal their breasts completely. The jewelry on their throats and wrists and arms was beautiful, delicate work of gold and enamel, and two of the women wore small aprons over their skirts that were masterworks of embroidery. Their hair was elaborately dressed, and the faces of the older women were heavily made up.

At first I thought that any of them might be the princess the men had spoken of, but after gazing at all of them, my eyes came back to the youngest one. Her clothing was simpler than that of her companions, and she wore no makeup except a touch of color on her lips and some eyeliner that made her big dark eyes look even larger. Her jewelry, though less elaborate than that of her companions, was marvelously made; I especially coveted a necklace, the links of which were leaping dolphins. All the women had pride and grace, but this youngest one had something else: The lift of her head and the set of her firm little chin spoke of authority.

She went straight to M'tano, who gave her the same salute he had given me. "You did all you could, M'tano," she said. "I grieve for your ship." Then she turned to me and said simply, "Greetings, Sister." She took my hands with the same gesture the woman of the thiasos of Dionysos had used; I wondered if it was only a coincidence. She looked into my eyes; I tried to meet those piercing dark eyes without flinching.

She looked at me for a long moment, then turned to the tall man with an impish smile. "You're a fool, Akono," she said. "This is no fisher girl—you could have told that by her hands if nothing else. But she's certainly not one of the People of the Sea, M'tano, and though there's something strange about her, I don't think she's an Olympian. Are you, my dear?" she asked, searching my face with those disquietingly intelligent eyes.

"No, my Lady," I said, my resolve not to speak melting before her directness. "But I'm here at this time and place because of some plan of Apollo's. I don't belong to this place, and I'm not sure what he wants of you—or of me. But I'll help you if I can. My name is Alice."

"Thank you, Aleesah," she said, and I noticed with a little pang that she softened my name in the same way that Nikos had. "I know that you're speaking the truth; that's a power that the women of our house have. Have you seen the god, spoken to him, or did he give you his message in some other way?"

"I have seen him and spoken to him," I said quietly, with a

feeling of relief that the power which she claimed to have—and which I did not doubt she had—would tell her I was speaking the truth.

"I envy you," she said. "I have always been curious about the gods and wished that I could see them face-to-face, as men and women of our house did in older days. But the gods appear rarely to us; the wise ones say the society of the gods is not good for mortals. When they do speak to us, the words of the immortals are hard for us to understand, but if they want something of us, they make *that* clear in their own time. Where did you see the god?"

"Up there on the slopes of the great mountain," I said, pointing to the gap in the hills where in my own day the modern village of Delphi could be seen. There was nothing visible there now, but a primitive village would not be so easy to see at a distance as the hotels and shops of modern Delphi.

"Then we must go to the place where the god spoke to you," said the princess decisively. "Where he spoke once he may speak again. Akono, see to supplies; we may get up there before dark, but we won't get back down. T'ne, you're a priestess; I'd like you with me if you feel you can make the climb. M'tano, I suppose you'll insist on going with me, but we don't need a large party. And pick the men from my guards; they haven't been working as hard as your sailors."

The two men saluted and went off to execute her orders. After the way the two of them had bickered earlier, their instant obedience said a great deal about the authority which rested in the slender figure of this dark-haired girl.

She now turned to me with a friendly smile and said, "You can't climb the hills in what you're wearing, Aleesah, but I don't think that anything my ladies or I have would fit you. Perhaps we can find a nice piece of material that you can use for a dress like that the mainland women wear. Let's see what we can find in my boxes."

But when we were helped down to the beach by respectful sailors, my eye was caught by a little bundle sitting near a rock on the edge of the water. There was a bag made of some woven material and a pottery jar. When I lifted the cover of the jar and found olives, I wasn't surprised to find that the bag held bread, cheese wrapped in some leaves, a pair of sandals, and a dress that fitted me. The dress was little more than two pieces of material fastened together at the shoulders and held at the waist with a sash. But there was some art in the cutting and shaping of the cloth, and when I slipped it on and belted it about me, it felt comfortable and seemed to fall in graceful folds.

"By our Mother, my Lady, will we have to wear clothing like that here?" asked the youngest of the ladies in waiting, shaking my confidence a little.

"Aleesah looks very pretty in it, and it will be a lot more practical on our walk than court dress," said the princess with a smile at me. "In fact, I think I'll wear my dancer's kilt for this walk, with a cloak if we meet any prudish mainlanders." She disappeared into the shelter and emerged in a few moments dressed only in a simple white kilt and short soft boots. "Dancer's dress," she said in response to my surprised look. "Have you heard of our Kaphtui bull dance?"

I remembered very vividly the fresco I had seen in Knossos of young men and women, dressed in only simple kilts, leaping over the horns of a great bull. Evidently the Cretan girl thought of this as a dance rather than as an act of bravery or an athletic feat. "Did you leap over the horns of the bull?" I asked in surprise, looking at her seemingly fragile form.

"Oh, yes, I was a leaper," she said simply. "All the king's children must take part in the dance, and every dancer wants to be one of the leapers. That's all in the past now, but as a former leaper I can still wear the kilt when I want to. Strictly speaking, the only women entitled to wear the kilt are the novices, the dancers for this year, and last year's dancers who are instructing the novices, but some of us who were leapers stretch out the privilege another year or two, until we bear children and no longer care to show so much flesh. Today I'll be glad of the privilege; once we get away from the sea breeze, it will be as hot as the inside of a fire mountain."

She was right about the heat; as we trudged up one foothill after another, each steeper than the last, sweat trickled down between my breasts, and the fairly heavy material of my dress began to stick to my back and my legs. I envied the princess her kilt and the other Cretan woman her open jacket, though not her bulky skirt.

At last we got near the hillside where the temple stood in my

time. Taking the easiest paths up the hill had brought us toward
the area of the Castalian Spring, and when I saw the cleft in the
hills where the spring came out, I told the princess that there was
good water there. We made a rest stop at the spring. I retrieved
my jar of olives from the soldier who had uncomplainingly carried
them for me and passed them around. Everyone exclaimed at their
size and delicious taste, and I felt a sort of vicarious pride in the
olives of Amphissa.

There had been a sort of picnic mood during our rest stop, but
as we approached the area where the shrine would stand, we fell
silent; all of us, I think, felt something in the place that made us
solemn and respectful. We moved more slowly and spoke with
lowered voices. The princess soon gestured for the party to stop
and said quietly, "Aleesah and I will go on alone. The rest of you
wait here." Again there were no protests, only obedience. I led the
princess in the direction of the Rock; I was sure I could recognize
that at any period of its history. I wondered what I could say if we
got there and nothing happened; but a familiar tingle began to
make itself felt in my body, and I thought that the Cretan princess
would not be disappointed in her wish to see a god face-to-face.

At last we stood by the Rock itself in the gathering dusk of
evening. The princess said half to herself, "This is a place where
the Mother has been invoked." She turned to me and said, "Can
you see how the cliffs above us and the hills opposite make a shape
like the horns of consecration? Or perhaps you do not know the
sign we Kaphtui use to mark a temple or shrine. We call them
horns, but it is a shape like that, half a circle cut out from a long,
squared stone. It is also like the top of the sacred double ax, and
there are other things said of it in the Mysteries." She paused and
went on. "If my two older sisters died, I would be the Ariadne and
also the priestess of Rhea, our Mother. I have had some instruction
in the things belonging to Her. I left orders for the sacrifices of
the white grain meal to be performed on the shore. We should
perform it here too."

But before she could say more, a great light burst forth on the
hillside above us. Great pillars of light, like searchlight beams,
reached to the sky above, columns of light where the columns of a

great temple would someday stand. I gasped; but the princess's face was calm and determined, and she made no move or sound.

A great voice sounded from the temple of light, a voice I recognized. "I am Apollo, son of Zeus and Leto," the voice said. "You men and women of Crete have been brought here to build and serve a great shrine to me here on this mountain. You will return no more to Crete, but you will have honor as my representatives and riches from the offerings men will bring to my shrine. I will not grudge you a generous share."

The princess spoke now, and though her voice was small compared to the voice of the god, it was firm and strong. "We are not children to be bribed with wealth and honor, Lord Apollo. I am Phane, daughter of M'nos the Sea King; those with me are priestesses and nobles of Kaphtu. If you want us to speak for you, Lord Apollo, we must know the one we speak for. Let me see you face-to-face."

The next moment the glowing form of the god stood before us. His face was stern, but there was grudging respect as he spoke to Phane. "We will not speak of wealth or honor then, daughter of M'nos," he said. "The blood of my uncle Poseidon runs in the veins of your house; it does not make you immortals, but it gives you much strength. There is a great work to be done here for the good of mortals. I ask if you will share in it, share in and know the plans of the Olympians."

Clever Apollo, I thought, to know the appeal that would reach this girl who had dreamed of seeing the gods face-to-face. Clever and ruthless, still moving his human pawns. Moving them well, too, for Phane said simply, "Yes, Lord Apollo, I will serve you in this, leave my homeland, and forget the bridegroom who awaits me in sandy Pylos. But remember, I am to be your priestess, not your slave."

Apollo's eyes seemed to be looking beyond us as he said, "You will be called the Pythia, in honor of the guardian of the shrine whom I had to slay because she was faithful to her trust. Once a year at first and more often in times to come, people will come to this shrine with questions for Apollo. I will be with you; you will see what I see and answer from my knowledge. It will be a heavy burden; can you bear it, mortal woman?" I wondered uneasily if Apollo was deciding all this or *seeing* it in the future.

Phane's voice was calm and remote as the voice of the god as she said, "Most of my people will stay with me, Lord Apollo, but you must let messengers go to my father and the man who will not now be my husband. We will build dwellings here on the mountain and keep ourselves separate from the people of these hills. You must let us have a shrine within your shrine to honor Posudi, the sea god, here; my captain and his mate are priests of Posudi. This place we will call Delphoi, the dolphins, so that we may remember how you brought us here to serve you."

Apollo nodded. "I will not grudge my uncle a corner of my shrine; the dolphins who brought you here are his creatures and served me by his favor. But no other gods must be honored within my shrine; even Rhea you must honor in another place now."

Made bold by Phane's example, I spoke up now. "Apollo, you told the Pythia that it was no use to fight what looms too large in the future to be changed. Dionysos will be honored here at Delphi, even within your shrine. His theater will stand beside your temple. So do not give Phane orders that cannot be carried out." Phane looked at me with a little smile, and I wondered again whether the handclasp she had given me when we first met meant that she, too, had followed Dionysos.

But there was cold anger in Apollo's voice as he said, "What you say may be true, girl, or it may not. It is not for you to give advice to the children of Zeus. Return to your own place; if you come here again, it will not be at *my* call." And suddenly Apollo was gone, and Phane, too; I stood before the Rock amid familiar ruins, in the cold light of dawn. There was sorrow in my heart because I had not been able to say good-bye to Phane; in the few hours I had known her I had come to love her. But most of all, there was cold fear in me that by my rash words I had cut myself off completely from a world of wonder and mystery that I had shared for a little while.

# CHAPTER TEN

After my abrupt return from the past it seemed that nearly everything that *could* go wrong *did*. In the first place I was spotted and very nearly caught when I left the site early that morning. Perhaps I should have waited until the site opened, but I was cold and tired and wanted to get to bed. I went over the fence and down the gravel road with a patrolling guard's whistle sounding in my ears. I had some luck, though: The guard was not close enough to identify me; one figure in T-shirt and jeans with longish hair looks pretty much like another. Then, when I got back to the hotel, Kyria Amalia popped out of her room and caught me coming up the stairs. My story about walking back from Itea after missing the last bus was not well received.

On Saturday, my second dinner with Nikos went badly. He had heard the story about the trespasser on the site from a friend who was a guard, and he had heard the story about my coming in early in the morning from Kyria Amalia. He didn't make any accusations, and he didn't suspect me of doing anything very dire. In a way it would have been easier if he had because then I could have played the injured innocent with conviction. What he did do was talk about the pride that Greeks had in their heritage and the fact that foreigners could get into serious trouble by disobeying Greek laws. He didn't do this in a threatening way, but he did make it clear that he was really concerned about the trouble I might get into if I were caught on the site when it was closed. When he finished, I felt about two feet tall and was wishing fervently that a Delphic earthquake would open up a crack in the earth for me to fall into. Feeling like that did *not* help me enjoy the rest of the dinner, nor did the news that Nikos would be busy with family business all week.

One small silver lining in this was that Nikos had evidently convinced Kyria Amalia that my reason for being out all night was an escapade of sneaking onto the site after it was closed. Kyria Amalia, who had suspected me of cavorting at the "deesko" and elsewhere with "those German boys," was considerably mollified. Breaking regulations out of zeal for my "studies" was plainly not a crime she took very seriously so long as no boys or discos were involved. I prayed fervently that injured vanity would keep Kurt Braun's mouth shut. The local gossip grapevine had already gotten word to Kyria Amalia that I had been with "German boys"; if she ever learned that I had sneaked onto the site with Kurt one night, her vivid imagination would provide her with a scenario for my all-night absence.

A temporary strategic withdrawal from Delphi seemed very much indicated. Besides that, I should really check in with my adviser, Professor Pennyquick, in Athens—or at least that's what I told myself. In her newly mellow mood Kyria Amalia agreed to hold my room for me for several days but not to charge me for any night that she could rent it to transients. Most of my possessions could be stored in a cupboard right in my room—a very high cupboard on top of the closet, which I had to get to by a rickety stepladder provided by Kyria Amalia. After getting my things up there, I concluded that anyone who was willing to go through all that for some clothes and books was welcome to them and stopped worrying about the fact that there was no lock on the cupboard.

Coming to Delphi, I had managed to cadge an empty seat on a tour bus which was bringing a group to Delphi, but for my trip back I took the regular Delphi–Athens bus service. It was crowded; but the seats were reserved, and the fact that I was traveling light—with only essentials for a couple of days' stay in Athens—made things easier. At the bus terminal in Athens people with lots of luggage were lining up for taxis, but I just hopped on a city bus to the center of town and then walked to the Plaka.

I went to the student hostel I'd stayed at before and cast myself on the mercy of the female half of the couple from New Zealand who managed the place for its owner. "Sally, can you give me any kind of bed for a couple of nights?" I pleaded. "I'll be glad to sleep on the roof if that's all you have."

She shook her head. "They won't let us let people sleep on the roof anymore; the tourist police are having one of their periodic crackdowns," she told me. "I'm sorry, Alice, the very best I can do is to let you have that little room on the second floor tonight, the one where the hall light comes in through the transom. And even that is rented tomorrow night."

"Thanks, Sally," I said. "I'll manage tomorrow night somehow. When will Professor Pennyquick be in?" I asked. "I have to see him about my project."

She looked concerned as she said, "Didn't you know? He's stopping over on Santorini after taking the summer group to Crete. He's not due here again for several days; the students have free time to do things on their own. Was he expecting you? He is a bit absentminded sometimes."

"No," I said, trying to hide my sinking feeling. "It's my own fault. I just assumed that he'd come back here after the Crete tour since he did in the spring. I'll have to think about whether to wait for him or to go back to Delphi and see him later. Are any of the people from my group still staying here? It would be nice to see *some* of them again."

She smiled sympathetically. Our group had been a good one on the whole, but we'd had our share of bores and crackpots. Tour members could evade them or, if worse came to worst, be rude to them, but the hostel staff had to be polite and cheerful. "All the students who are still here are off one place or another," she said. "But Professor Pierce is still here; you'll probably see her at breakfast."

"Oh, thanks," I said, a little dubiously. Professor Augustus Pennyquick, who was Gus to all his students, had been running these programs for Western Pacific University for several years; he was in the classics department at Pacific. This year the codirector had been Athena Pierce, a philosophy professor at Pacific who had been on one of the earlier tours with her husband and sister, not as a director but just as part of the group. I had taken only one class from her during the program and the rest from Gus Pennyquick.

Gus, who was easygoing and friendly, had been a favorite with everyone; people tended to take their troubles to him. Athena Pierce was a brilliant teacher, but she could have a sharp tongue on occasion and had tended to keep students at a distance. Apart from a few friends or former students who had come on the tour because she was going to be codirector, most group members had respected rather than liked her. I had somewhat mixed feelings about her myself.

As a successful female academic she was an obvious role model for me, but I wasn't sure I really wanted to be like her. There was a touch of arrogant certainty about her that might have been the defensive armor of a woman making her way in what was still largely a man's world but that made some in the group rather glad when she occasionally made a mistake or showed a human weakness, such as drinking a bit too much at dinner or getting lost taking us to a site in Athens. To do her justice, though, she was generally nice to the people in the group who were just ignorant or boring and showed her arrogant streak only to people who had a touch of arrogance themselves—including me, I guess. I suddenly realized that in some ways she reminded me a little of Apollo.

I didn't see her that night; to save money, I filled up on cheap and delicious vegetarian food at the Eden restaurant, then went to bed early. I woke late the next morning and went down to breakfast just before they stopped serving it. It was late enough that Athena Pierce and I were the only ones in the breakfast room. We chatted a bit about what each of us had been doing since the group broke up, and then she gave me an opening. "Sally told me that you came to see Gus and missed him because of his stopover on Santorini. Is there anything I can help you with?" she said.

I hesitated, then said, "You read science fiction, don't you? In one of your lectures you used some examples—"

"I've never been known to write the stuff," she said gravely but with a little twinkle in her gray-green eyes. "Do you have a problem that relates to science fiction?"

"Well, it's time travel really," I said, floundering a bit. "If someone went back into the past and then they or . . . somebody . . . did something that made the future different—I mean, the future then that's our present—could the whole world as it is now just . . . vanish?"

She raised an eyebrow. "I'm not sure how you got into this by studying Delphic history—oh, yes, I suppose I do. If you assume that the oracle made true prophecies, you get into the whole free will–foreknowledge thing and from there into time travel, okay. Well, the answer to your question depends on the theory of Time you buy into—whether it's a past-future view or a future-future view."

She paused. "Think of it in this way," she said slowly. "Ordinarily we think of the past as something we *can't* change and the future as something that we can. You and I have already had breakfast together; commonsensically we can't change that fact. We might or might not have lunch or dinner together; common sense says that's up to us. It depends on what *we* decide to do. Now a determinist would say that we can't change the future any more than we can change the past; that's what I call a past-past view. Either a past-future view or a past-past view gives you one kind of answer to questions about time travel, which is that if you go back at all, you can't change anything. If I go back in time and try to kill my grandmother before she gives birth to my mother, something or other will stop me; since, in fact, my grandmother *wasn't* killed, I can't kill her. Get it?"

I nodded, and she went on. "Now, the other view is much more interesting. It says that the past *can* be changed and since the future depends on the past to some extent, changes in the past will change the future. Suppose you want to make sure you won't have lunch with me today. You go back and change the past, so you never came to Athens today; therefore, you can't have lunch with me in Athens. That's what I call a future-future view; the past is just as changeable as the future. It goes against common sense, but so do some scientific theories that are almost certainly true. And for my money, a future-future view makes the best time-travel stories; it allows for time travel to make a difference. On a past-future or past-past view the end of the story is already set; you didn't change the past, so you can't change it."

"Could you have a future-past view?" I asked. "The past changeable and the future not?"

She smiled, pleased with me. "Very good. It's a theoretical possibility, but it's hard to make sense of. If the past affects the future, how *could* the past change and the future not? But raising the possibility shows that you're thinking."

I said slowly, "Someone said to me that you could change the past, but after a while the future would be the same anyway. Like damming a stream; after a way it flows back into the original channel."

Athena nodded, her face thoughtful. "That's a good analogy," she said, "and it makes a lot of sense. Take World War One, for instance; if someone hadn't assassinated that particular archduke at Sarajevo, the war would probably have started in some other way and gone on pretty much the same. But there would always be the possibility that a seemingly trivial change in the past would change the future in a major way."

"Then *our* present *could* just vanish if someone changed the past?" I asked.

"Well, here you're getting into an area where you have only the speculations of science fiction writers," said Athena Pierce. "Some have speculated that *every* possibility is realized, somewhere in a sort of multidimensional time. But that's really a very depressing view; think of all the horrible possibilities that could be realized— a Nazi victory in World War Two, for instance. Other writers have speculated that if you could interfere in the past, you'd create a new time track, so to speak, but the old one would also continue to exist. And then there are writers who think that a whole range of possibilities, a whole present time *could* just cease to exist. In lots of time-travel stories, some kind of time police works to keep that from happening."

My head was going around from the effort to think all this through. "But which of these views you've been telling me about is *true*?" I asked.

Athena shrugged. "That's a philosophical question," she said, "and it can only be answered, if it can be answered at all, by philosophical arguments based on the data that experience gives us. Experience seems to show that the commonsense, past-future view is true; we never succeed in changing the past, but we can affect what will happen in the future. But if someone actually traveled in time, we'd have to rethink our theories in light of his or her experience."

I sighed. All this was not a great deal of help in my present perplexities. "Could I change the subject?" I asked. "Do you think that there's any reality at all to the stories of the Greek gods, like Apollo and Dionysos, for instance?"

She gave me a rather peculiar glance. "Have you read either of my novels?" she asked. I shook my head; I hadn't even known that she wrote novels. She went on. "The fact is, you've hit on a sort of hobbyhorse of mine. I wrote a fantasy novel based on Greek mythology, then a sequel to it. I used the premise that the Greek gods were real and that they were basically of human stock, but with what some people call psionic powers—telepathy, precognition, and so on. I tied this up with a sort of parabiblical mythology you get in both Judaism and Christianity, about angels taking human form and interbreeding with humans. There are some biblical passages that seem to support that idea, but it's not part of mainstream theology in either Judaism or Christianity. Tolkien uses the idea in the *Silmarillion*, by the way, which is what gave me the idea."

She paused and looked thoughtfully out the window. "Now, mind you," she said slowly, "I don't take the idea really seriously; I don't give it what Tolkien called primary belief in his essay 'On Fairy Stories.' But it makes a lot of sense of a good many things in Greek mythology and history. It's an alternative speculative hypothesis. I won't put it any more strongly than that. But there's no real evidence for it."

"What if someone had evidence?" I asked, and there must have been something in my voice that showed how serious I was because she looked at me curiously.

"What's happened, Alice? Did you travel back in time and meet a Greek god?" she asked lightly. Then, as she saw my reaction to that, she said sharply, "Young woman, are you trying to pull my leg?"

Suddenly it all had to come out. We sat there for what seemed hours, while our coffee grew cold and Sally and her husband cast curious glances at us from the kitchen, as I poured out all that had happened to me since my arrival at Delphi: Apollo and Dionysos, Nikos and Kurt Braun, Kyria Amalia and the Cretan princess Phane, all mixed up together.

When I finished, Athena Pierce ran her fingers through her hair and looked at me in perplexity. "Oh, I believe you, Alice, in the sense that I believe that you're perfectly sincere," she said. "I don't think that all this is an elaborate hoax, and I don't think that you've gone crazy or anything. But believing that all this actually happened is another thing. You may very well have had some very vivid dreams or hallucinations, based on a lot of half-remembered things you've read about Delphi. I could give you a source for about ninety percent of the details you've given me; a lot of the stuff about Apollo is in the Homeric Hymn to Pythian Apollo, for instance."

I started to protest, and she raised a hand. "I didn't say you got it from there. I just say it's there; from your point of view you could call it corroborative evidence. But there's no physical evidence. No one saw you vanish into the past or come back from the past. You didn't bring anything from the past, and you didn't even lose anything there."

She frowned. "This business of your clothing and possessions changing to suit the time period bothers me. It makes sense in one way; if some power brought you back in time, it might try to minimize the disturbing effects of your presence in the past by changing your appearance so that you'd fit in better. But it means that one kind of physical evidence is ruled out; we're not going to dig up a tenth-century B.C. tomb and find an Adidas running shoe marked 'Alice Grant' among the tenth-century relics. And I suppose that it might work the other way; if you tried to bring back an authentic ancient tetradrachma, it might turn into a plain old modern five-drachma piece, with the extra drachma for inflation." She grinned at me, and I had to smile back.

"I suppose," she said slowly, "that in theory your movements could be traced; it could be shown you didn't get from the site to Amphissa, or from Itea to the site, in any ordinary way. But it's awfully hard to prove a negative, and in fact, you *could* have walked from Itea to Delphi during the course of the night without anyone's seeing you or got a lift from Delphi to Amphissa in a car that can't be traced. I don't know if there'd be time, but I presume you don't want to get Kurt Braun and Nikos Petrides together to compare times."

I shook my head with a rueful laugh, and she smiled absently.

"Remind me to introduce you to a friend of mine who married a Greek and have her tell you about what she calls the Greek boyfriend thing. It's a lot more complex than it seems. But I'm mixing your problems about boys with the problem about how real your experiences were," she went on. "*I'd* like some proof one way or another whether this is real or just a vivid mental experience. You're sure in your own mind that it's all real; what you want to do is get back to that reality, have more of these experiences. Well, I'm not sure I can give you any advice about that. If it is real, you probably can't *make* it happen, just wait for it to happen to you: put yourself in the right places at the right times." She paused and then said half-reluctantly, "Well, I do have one crazy kind of suggestion. You've tried the gods of Delphi, but . . . do you know who the temple down by the Tholos was dedicated to?"

"Why . . . it's a temple of Athena," I said.

"That's right," she said with a smile. "My namesake, the goddess Athena. You've tried the gods of Delphi. Why not give the goddess a try?"

# CHAPTER

# ELEVEN

One result of my pouring out my problems to Athena Pierce was, I think, that she felt a certain responsibility for me. When I told her that Sally couldn't give me a room for the next night, Athena got Doug, Sally's husband, to move an extra bed into Athena's own room for a couple of nights, making it easier for us to talk privately as well as solving my lodging problem. Since she was staying at the hostel for a while while she did some research on modern Greek philosophy, she had fixed up her room a little with a few posters and pictures and knickknacks. It made me realize how impersonal most of the rooms I'd been living in during my stay in Greece had been, and I decided to fix up my room at Kyria Amalia's a bit, including getting a good bedside lamp like Athena's to make reading in bed easier.

Athena had appointments during the day, and I had to get to a good library for some more reading on my long-neglected research project. I had decided that I might as well carry on with normal life as much as I could; simply sitting around waiting to see if the Path would open for me again would make it even harder. And since my project involved reading up on the myths and legends of Delphi as well as its history, I was constantly running into things that reminded me of my experiences in the past.

I was also reminded of Nikos quite a lot, by young men I saw on the streets who resembled him in one way or another. Then the night before I returned to Delphi, Athena gave me some food for thought by arranging a dinner for us with her friend Judy, an American writer who had settled down in Greece some years ago.

Judy was involved with an organization that helped foreigners in Greece (especially women) with a variety of problems, and she had a fund of stories, some funny and some horrifying, about the problems you could run into living in Greece.

I liked Judy at once; she seemed to have a lot of common sense and compassion as well as an active and somewhat wild sense of humor. She also won my heart by being an enthusiast for some of my favorite books, including childhood favorites such as the Oz books. So when she did start talking about the "Greek boyfriend thing," I was prepared to put a lot of stock in her ideas.

"As you've discovered," she said dryly, "if a foreign girl is even passable-looking, the Greek men are charming, attentive, and very single-minded. You can't blame them in one way. Most Greek girls of their age are very well protected, and if they did manage to seduce one, she would have male relatives who would take it with deadly seriousness—and I mean deadly. So any young Greek who wants what most young men want has fantasies about the free-and-easy foreign girl, who's outside the protection of Greek society. Don't misunderstand me—you're far safer from actual rape than in most countries, but the salesmanship is terrific." She gave a rather bawdy chuckle.

Then she looked at me more seriously. "But I understand from 'Thena that you're involved with a young man who may have something more permanent in mind than a summer affair. That's a whole different thing and much more complicated. The whole attitude changes. When my husband and I were going out together and he stopped being demonstrative in public, I realized that he was thinking of marriage. How has this young man been treating you?"

I tried to describe my few brief meetings with Nikos, realizing as I did how little in one way there had been to them. But Judy looked grave. "It sounds as if he's serious," she said. "He's been courting you rather as he might a Greek girl. But the big giveaway is that he's discussed you with his mother. He's thinking of marriage, all right, whether you are or not."

"Of course I'm not," I said, feeling flattered and pleased by the idea that Nikos wanted to marry me, but a little panicky too.

Judy grinned. "Greek men have a good many old-fashioned male attitudes: Women are either the kind you marry or the *other* kind. Since he's decided you're not the *other* kind, your friend's thoughts have turned to marriage."

She sighed. "I'm married to a Greek myself," she said, "and very happily, thank you. But it's a difficult business for a foreign girl to marry a Greek. For one thing, you're not even legally married in the eyes of the law unless you marry in the Orthodox Church. For another, women have almost no legal rights. For instance, it's illegal for a wife in Greece to spend a night away from home without her husband's permission. If our organization helps a battered wife leave home, we're committing a criminal act in the eyes of the law."

She frowned thoughtfully. "But that's not the biggest thing you have to contend with. There's a whole pattern of life for Greek men that involves their spending a great deal of their time away from home, with other men—at *kafeneions*, at taverns, lots of places. The wife is left alone with the children, or with her mother-in-law, or the husband's unmarried sister. And even if a Greek man was crazy enough about you to break the pattern, he'd be hurting himself socially and professionally; the other men wouldn't respect him. It's a big thing to fight. I don't fight it myself; as a writer I can put all that time by myself to good use. But if you have American expectations about togetherness with your husband, you'll have to cut them way down, if not forget them entirely, even with the most enlightened and liberated Greek husband. With most Greek men you can just forget togetherness entirely."

Riding back to Delphi on the bus the next day, I thought about what Judy had said. According to her, Nikos was probably thinking in terms of marriage. Despite what I had told Judy, was I? Not seriously, I told myself; I was too young, had too many plans for things to do before I married. But there was something very special about Nikos, and I wouldn't kid myself that I hadn't had some daydreams. I certainly didn't want to stop seeing Nikos, but would it be fair to encourage him if I didn't want to marry and he did? I came to the somewhat comforting conclusion that unless and until Nikos declared himself, there wasn't much I could do and that meantime, I could continue to go out with him—if he asked me.

Athena Pierce's ideas disturbed me in a rather different way. In our late-night talks in her room before we went to sleep she had told me about all kinds of science-fictional treatments of time. There was a story by Ray Bradbury in which a time traveler stepped on a butterfly and changed the whole course of history, for example. Did I really want to travel again into the past, knowing that there *might* be a risk of some trivial action of mine changing the world in some unforeseeable way? By the time I got back to Delphi my feelings about finding the Path open again were just as ambivalent as my feelings about seeing more of Nikos.

I found flowers and a message that Nikos hoped to see me soon waiting at the hotel when I got back. I reflected that if I had been frantically longing to see him, there probably would have been no message. Things you want often start almost chasing you just when you aren't sure you want them anymore. Of course, that didn't apply to the Path—or did it?

I had quite a nice dinner at a little family taverna called Zorba's a street up from the main street, and then I firmly went to bed early, to Kyria Amalia's evident approval. But as a result, I woke up practically at first light, long before breakfast, and decided to walk out to the site. I looked longingly at the firmly locked gate, but since it had been early morning when I was nearly caught before, I didn't even dare to stop. The little café near the Castalian Spring wasn't open yet, and I kept on walking, toward the Tholos area.

When I got there, the site was deserted, and I walked slowly to the area where Athena's temple had stood for centuries. How did you invoke a goddess? I decided it was no use gritting my teeth and trying to project a thought across the centuries. I sat down, closed my eyes, and simply waited.

It was very quiet, but birds were singing. There was a pleasant early-morning smell, mostly a piney sort of smell from some trees and bushes nearby. I could feel a slightly chilly breeze on my face. I sat there for a long time, just waiting. Gradually the noise of birdsong died away and the light grew stronger on my closed eyelids. I could no longer smell the pines or feel the breeze. When I opened my eyes at last, all I could see was a blank, featureless gray; it was like looking into a gray morning sky. I looked around, seeing nothing but gray, and when I looked directly in front of me again, there was a woman standing before me.

She wore a simple white dress of classical cut, and her feet, I think, were bare, though a sort of mist rising from the ground made it hard to see. Her dark blond hair was arranged in a simple style that would not have seemed out of place in most times or places. Her chin was firm but rounded, her nose long and straight, and her eyes were the same clear cold gray as the blank gray background behind her. I had no doubt that this was Athena, whom the poets called "gray-eyed," and "clear-eyed." I felt an awe I had not felt when I had seen Apollo, even when I had seen Dionysos, but it was a quiet awe; all emotions seemed muted here.

"This a place outside of all times," said the goddess quietly. "Nothing you do here can affect your times or mine. Your head is full of the dreams of your storytellers. Don't be afraid; the lines of time are not easily bent by mortals."

"Are we just water bugs on the Stream of Time then?" I asked, a little bitterly.

She shook her head with a slow smile. "That's a poet's image— my half brother is a poet as well as other things. Like all such figures, it has some likenesses and some unlikenesses to what it images. In that image the water bugs are alive and the stream is not. It would be true in a way to say that there is no stream, only intertwined lives. Your life has become intertwined with other lives in a strange way. Now you have to decide whether that intertwining will continue."

I looked at her in amazement. "You mean it's up to me?" I asked.

She nodded, her face grave. "Up to now your consent has been unconscious," she said. "The call that 'Pollo sent down the Path could bring only someone who was deeply willing to come, who would have said yes to the call if it had been put into words. But now we, the Olympians, are asking for your help, and your consent must be conscious."

"Yes, of course, if I'd been asked, I'd have been delighted with the idea of going back in time and seeing the beginnings of Delphi," I said, "but I don't see how I can help you . . . Olympians."

"Do your people still remember a tale our people tell about a mouse that helped a lion?" she asked with a smile. "But the help we want of you is not a small thing, and it is not without danger for you. Not all of us from Olympus always remember it, but the powers we have are given to us for the sake of you mortals, to fight against certain Powers who would enslave you if they could. It is a fight in which strategy can be more important than mere strength, as it often is in war. Because you come from where you do, our enemies can neither understand you nor guess what you will do, and you are protected from them in ways we could not protect any mortals of our days. By putting you into a situation, we can confuse our enemies' plans and seize an advantage."

I looked at her searchingly and summoned up the courage to say, "How do I know that the things you might want me to do are really for the benefit of us ordinary people—mortals? How do I know that your enemies are our enemies?"

She looked at me with those clear gray eyes and said quietly, "You do not *know*. You must trust us. Not everything done in the name of the Olympians was done by us; not all tales told of us are true. But we are remembered in your day; you told 'Pollo so when you first met him. All I can do is to ask you to judge by what is remembered of us whether we were good or evil, friends or enemies to mortals."

For someone like myself, who had always loved the "glory that was Greece," it was an easy question to answer. "If the Olympians are real—and it seems you are—we owe you more than we can ever repay. I'm willing to do what I can to help pay that debt," I said. "What do you want me to do?"

There was new warmth in her smile as she said, "That is something our enemies will never understand: that one person will help another from gratitude or love. They trust no one they cannot dominate. That is what has led to the trouble in which we need your help. 'Pollo promised the Cretan princess that she would be his priestess, not his slave. He has kept that word to her and her successors; they serve him freely. But since they are free, they can choose not to serve; they can betray their mission. The Dark Powers have wanted for a long time to take over the oracle of Delphi for their own purposes, to use it to mold this land and people to their own image, as they have partly done with some of the great and cruel empires to the east."

She paused and went on with sorrow in her voice. "But as often happens, their contempt for their human tools spoiled their plans. They intended to dominate the Pythia who betrayed her trust. Instead, they destroyed her mind. Now a new Pythia must be chosen, and it is not easy to find one whose mind will stand what a Pythia must undergo. Those who must choose will come to my temple, as they will come to other places where there are women who serve the Olympians, for a true priestess has the type of mind they need, one able to see a little further into our realm than most mortals can."

She looked into my eyes and said simply, "None of the women who serve me there and then is strong enough for the task. You are. But that does not mean that it will be simple or easy for you to withstand the attacks which will be made on you. If your will falters, you could be overcome, and we cannot be sure of saving you. You might never return to your own time, or return with your mind broken."

Even in that place where all emotion seemed stilled, an icy wave of fear went through me at those words. But something else rose to meet that fear: a courage I did not know I possessed. "What will I have to do?" I asked.

"There is a girl not unlike you who serves me at my temple near Delphi," the goddess said. "You will take her place, and very soon the priests from 'Pollo's temple will come, seeking someone to serve as the Pythia until they can find a permanent replacement. My chief priestess will offer you, and I think that they will accept. After that, it is hard to know what will happen; you confuse our sight as well as the sight of our enemies. But if you hold hard to the truth as you know it, our enemies can be overcome. Will you do it then?"

"I will," I said, and even in that moment it occurred to me that I had chosen the words the bride says in the marriage ceremony.

"Thank you," said the goddess quietly, and then her gray eyes seemed to grow into two gray pools into which I plunged deep, deep before I lost consciousness.

# CHAPTER TWELVE

I awoke on a narrow cot, in a simple whitewashed room with only a washstand and chair for furnishings, apart from the bed I lay on. I had been sleeping in a sort of sack with holes for my arms and head. Hanging on the wall was a dress of the kind I had worn on my previous experiences in the past and two pieces of cloth which evidently served as underclothing. I stripped off the sack, washed with the aid of the basin and pitcher of cold water on the washstand, and managed to dress, though the undergarments felt a bit insecure. Just then there was a scratching on the door of the room. "Come in," I called, and a short dark girl with a friendly, cheerful face came in.

"Oh, Phemonoë," she said with a little giggle. "All the time you've been here and you can't remember to say, 'Enter in Athena's name.' And your hair not done either. Where's your comb?" She seized it from the washstand and soon had my hair fixed in a sort of knot at the back of my head, chattering all the time. "No chanting this morning," she said, "not even the morning offering. Some men are here talking with the lady Ataia—priests, by the look of them, of him up-the-hill. We're all to assemble in front of the temple. What do you think it's all about?"

She plunged into gossip and speculation, but I knew very well what it was about. Athena had wasted no time; the men from "up-the-hill" must be here to seek a replacement for the unfortunate Pythia who had lost her mind. Just as well, because I hadn't the slightest idea what the duties of a junior priestess in a temple of Athena were—I presumed that's what I was. I wondered if to the dark-haired girl I looked just as her friend did and how Athena had

managed that. Lucky the girl was a chatterbox who wasn't suspicious
when I didn't respond appropriately to her chatter—or was that
arranged by Athena too?

We came out of the long, low building behind the temple which
held the room I had awaked in; from the glimpses I had through
open doors of other rooms like mine, the building seemed to be a
sort of dormitory for the priestesses. The temple's columns soared
above us as we walked around the front of the temple, but they
were wood, not stone. I must still have been far back in history,
before stone columns replaced the original tree-trunk columns in
Greek temples.

The wood of the columns had been allowed to weather to a delicate
gray, but the bases and capitals were gaily painted. On the triangular
area above the columns and below the wooden roof, some sort of
picture was painted in bright colors. I longed to stop and stare at
it, but that would be out of character for the girl I was supposed
to be. Across a little grassy area, about where the Tholos would
stand, was a small circular structure with a conical roof and wooden
columns, which reminded me of picnic shelters in parks at home.
A slender plume of smoke coming from the roof increased the
resemblance.

About half a dozen women of various ages, all dressed in simple
white dresses, stood talking quietly in front of the temple. An older
woman with a strikingly handsome face and an air of dignity and
command stood talking to two men, also dressed simply in white.
The older man was white-haired and bearded; he looked both kind
and wise. The younger man with him had a sharp nose, and his
bearing and gestures indicated a fussy self-importance that con-
trasted sharply with the natural dignity of the older man and woman.

When the older woman saw my companion and me, she shot me
a sharp glance. I met her eyes for a moment and felt that she saw
me as I was, not as the girl I was supposed to be. She called out
to all of us in a deep, melodious voice, "The servants of the lord
Apollo have need of our help. If you will make a line as we do for
the morning offering, they would like to look at each of you."

It looked as if the lineup were in order of seniority, and even
my dark-haired companion took her place ahead of me; all I had
to do was fall in at the end of the line. The white-haired priest of

Apollo walked slowly down the line, peering into faces and gently touching each woman on the shoulder. When he came to me, he looked into my eyes for a long time, then brought up his hand to my shoulder. Before he had even touched me, I felt a sharp tingle, like an electric shock. It was so unexpected that I stepped backward, giving a little gasp.

The priest himself looked startled, but he spoke in a deep, soothing voice. "I am sorry to frighten you, my child. Have no fear, it will not harm you; it is a holy thing from the sanctuary of the lord Apollo." I saw that he had been holding some small object wrapped in cloth in the hand with which he had touched each woman. He turned to the older priestess who had told us to line up. "This is the girl you told me of, Lady Ataia?" he asked. She nodded, and he turned to me. "Lady Ataia tells me that your name is Phemonoë. That is a name of good omen, for it is the name of our first Pythia."

"But surely her name was Phane," I said before I thought.

"True enough, Bright Lady," he said with a puzzled look. "She took the other name later. But I had not thought that the ladies of Athena knew so much of our history."

Lady Ataia laughed. "You are forgetting the roots, both the old speech and the tongue of this land, my Lord Telontas," she said. "*Phane* means 'Golden Lady,' a very proper name in the old tongue for a daughter of M'nos. But *Phemonoë* is in the tongue of this land and means no more than 'prophetic mind'; it was the name given to Lady Phane in the days after she became the Pythia. We have not forgotten our roots in Kaphtu any more than you have, my Lord. And you need not call our Phemonoë Bright Lady; she is only a novice and has not made her vows to Athena yet. And that will make your plan simpler. I will leave you to talk with the girl. Ladies, we have not yet made the morning offering. Come with me." She shot me a warning glance as she bustled the other priestesses away, and I realized that the piece of information I had let slip was not something a priestess of Athena would normally know, though she had covered up for me beautifully.

At any rate, Telontas seemed to have forgotten his puzzlement and now turned to me with gentle courtesy. "My dear, I speak to you with the permission of Lady Ataia," he said. "We of Apollo's temple are in need of help from the ladies who serve his sister. Our

Pythia has suffered a grave illness and can no longer do her duties. But today is the seventh day of the month, and many folk, great and humble, are waiting for word from the god. If you would consent to lend your gifts to us for this one day, you would save the temple from embarrassment and many inquirers from disappointment. Your help would further cement the bond between Apollo's shrine and this temple of Athena before the shrine."

"I am willing to help, my Lord, and most honored," I said. "But I know nothing of the service of Apollo."

"She is right, my Lord," broke in the younger priest. "How can this mere child, who already serves Athena, serve our Lord, Apollo, fittingly? There are many of our own girls, who have fed the sacred fire and observed the rituals, who can do the ritual of the beans for the ordinary inquirers and give some sort of answer to the king."

"You blaspheme, Pertax," said Telontas sternly. "Unless the god inspires the choice of beans, the lot ritual has no validity; would you send the simple people away with worthless answers merely because they are poor? And 'some sort of answer to the king' indeed! Even aside from the insult to the god, do you think the king will be easily fobbed off with some riddling answer? You saw what happened the other day when he insisted on an answer even though all the signs said that the god was not ready to speak!"

Telontas turned to me and said quietly, "My child, none of the women who serve our shrine have your gift. You have it to a greater degree than I have ever seen; no Pythia has ever reacted as strongly as you did in the test. The rituals are simple and easily learned: Most inquiries are answered by your choosing a black or white bean from the bowl on the tripod. But if the god puts anything in your mind to say, tell it to the priest on duty in the old speech of our homeland, which we still speak among ourselves. He will interpret it for the inquirer; it is not always wise to tell them all the god says. If it is an important message, the poet who serves the shrine will put it into verses so that it may be more easily remembered and repeated, to the glory of the god."

I was silent for a moment; I suppose that he thought that I was timidly shrinking from the task. In fact, my decision had already been made, and I was silent because my mind was racing. Of course, this was the explanation for the so-called meaningless babbling of the Pythia; she spoke in an old form of Cretan, preserved as a ceremonial language, and spoken by the priests and priestesses among themselves. That still left a good deal of latitude to the priest who interpreted her words; a message unwelcome to a powerful inquirer could be softened, for instance.

*"Katalavenes Danaika?"* said the younger priest suddenly. I turned a puzzled face to him; I thought at first he was asking me if I spoke Greek, but he had said not *"Hellenika"* but another word. He gave a little smile at my incomprehension, and a suspicion crossed my mind.

Telontas frowned at him. "Lady Ataia told me she is from Kaphtu and speaks the old tongue as a native," he said. "We can give her the questions in her own language, and it does not matter if she cannot understand our interpretation of her answers." Yet it might matter a great deal if the answer interpreted were not the same as the answer given.

"My Lord Telontas, I am willing to do this, but will you yourself be the priest who interprets for me?" I asked. Pertax started to protest, but Telontas silenced him with a wave of his hand.

"If it will help you, my child, I will be happy to serve as 'prophet,'" he said gravely. "There is no ritual reason I should not; it is merely that as I grow older, I tend to leave it to the younger men. But in this unusual case it might be very wise for me to do it." His eyes rested on Pertax, and he frowned slightly.

There was a certain amount of fuss before we could leave the temple of Athena. When the priestesses had finished their chanting in the temple, I shared with them hearth cakes and steaming herb tea, evidently their usual breakfast. Then each one embraced me, and the lady Ataia wrapped me in a cloak of her own with richly embroidered borders. "For the honor of the temple," she said with a smile, but her hug was more affectionate than formal.

Finally we set off up the hill and before long had reached the familiar gorge of the Castalian Spring. "If you insist on using this girl, Lord Telontas," said Pertax huffily, "we will save time by having her do her lustrations at the spring now."

Telontas frowned thoughtfully. "Yes, I suppose so," he said grudgingly, "though it is hardly fitting with no female attendants." He turned to me. "You need not bathe yourself in the usual way,"

he said. "A mere ceremonial washing will do." He led me into the
gorge to where the water from the spring was caught in a gracefully
shaped pool, really quite large enough to bathe in. But the water
was icy cold, and I was just as glad not to have to immerse myself
in it. Smiling a little to myself, I knelt by the pool and washed
my face and wrists three times, then drank from my cupped hands,
three deep drafts. "Well done," said Telontas. "Come, my child."

We walked slowly up a dirt road until we came to a place that
was more or less where the gate of the site was in my time. Here
there was a gap in the trees and bushes which had hidden the upper
part of the hill from me, and I looked up and saw the Temple,
standing where the ruins were in my time, white and beautiful but
touched with brilliant color here and there. The few buildings
around it were low and simple; evidently I had come to a time
before the shrine was crowded with monuments and treasures from
almost every major Greek city-state.

There weren't great crowds of people either, at least this early
in the morning. Everyone I could see was busy at some kind of job:
sun-burned men in dark tunics sweeping paths and pruning trees;
white-clad men sluicing off the altar in front of the Temple with
buckets of water. I watched a bucket carrier go up the hill above
the Temple to refill his buckets; the spring where he got the water
seemed to be roughly where the little cistern stood in my time.

I heard the bleating of goats from somewhere near the Temple.
I remembered with an unpleasant feeling that there would be animal
sacrifices but told myself not to be squeamish. I was happy enough
to eat meat dishes when the animals were slaughtered out of my
sight. Here in these times animals were ceremonially killed in honor
of the gods, and some portions burned, but the rest of the meat
was cooked and eaten by the priests and people. For many of the
poorer people, the meat sent from the Temple on festival days was
the only meat in their diet.

Telontas led me straight up the steps into the front entrance of
the Temple, where he dismissed Pertax rather sharply and gave
some instructions to men who seemed to be minor priests or temple
attendants. I looked around me at the anteroom of the Temple,
wishing that I could go outside and gape at the brightly painted
relief sculpture above the door. I wasn't sure whether the columns

of this temple were wood or stone; even at the height of Delphi's wealth and power I knew that they had been of rough local stone plastered over to look like marble. These columns were smooth and white and showed no divisions into the sections called drums, characteristic of stone columns, but plastering could account for that.

The column bases I could see did look like stone, and there was a squarish stone column in the antechamber. With a little thrill I puzzled out the letters and read the two Delphic maxims:

Know thyself
Nothing in excess

Telontas turned back to me and led me into the inner part of the Temple. We entered an extraordinary chamber like a small auditorium, with the back part of the room filled with rows of benches. The front of the room had a sort of holy clutter which reminded me of an old-fashioned Catholic or Orthodox church, crowded with statues or icons. There was one statue here of what I guessed was gilded wood; the sculptor had caught something of Apollo's arrogant certainty in the stance of the young god with the bow, but the face was nothing like the real face of Apollo. Near the statue on stands were a lyre made of a tortoise shell and a cluster of what seemed to be armor.

On the other side of the room was an egg-shaped stone on a stone base. This must be the omphalos stone, which was supposed to mark the center of the world, but it bore very little resemblance to any of the several stones which modern archaeologists had identified as the omphalos. This stone looked to me as if it might be a meteorite.

Behind the statue of Apollo and the omphalos stone were what looked like fresh-cut branches of laurel, stuck into some kind of holders so that they made a wall of greenery at the end of the room. But the most extraordinary object was what stood in the middle of the front of the room, down a little flight of shallow steps. It was a little hut with a curtained door. From its position in the Temple I was willing to bet that it was built directly on the rough gray rock where I had emerged on my first trip into the past.

As I stared at the hut, Telontas spoke from behind me. "Presently, my child, you must enter into that sacred enclosure and await the coming of the god. His coming is hard to bear at the best of times, but strange things have been happening of late. You are so young, my child, so young. I am afraid for you—very much afraid."

# CHAPTER
# THIRTEEN

I spun around and faced Telontas. "What happened to the previous Pythia?" I asked bluntly.

He hesitated, then decided to answer me. "We have a test to see if the god is present and prepared to speak," he said, "a test that doesn't depend on human beings, who may deceive themselves into believing what they want to believe. We bring one of the sacrificial goats into this chamber. An experienced eye can tell if the animal feels the signs of the god's presence, but to make it obvious, we sprinkle the goat with cold water. If the god is present, the cold water is enough to make the animal go into a fit of violent shuddering. It's very distinctive; no one could possibly mistake it for any normal animal behavior. When the goat doesn't shiver, we can be sure that it's no use bringing in the Pythia. But a few days ago a very powerful neighboring king came insisting on asking the god a question. We offered him the lot oracle, using the two beans, but he insisted on a spoken message from the god."

The old priest looked both unhappy and ashamed. "We *told* him that the god speaks, if he speaks at all, only on the seventh day of the month. Certain . . . threats . . . were made by the king, and we reluctantly agreed to try. Of course, the goat did not tremble, but he insisted that we douse the poor beast with more and more water, until the miserable creature did begin to shiver, though in quite a different way from the shudders that indicate the presence of the god. When the goat shivered, the king insisted we bring in the Pythia, and we were forced to do it."

Telontas looked away from me as if he could not meet my eyes. "As soon as the poor girl tried to speak, I knew that what we had done was terribly wrong. When ceremonies belonging to the Olympians are wrongly or lightly performed, this gives an opening to older, darker Powers." I thought of the way in which Satanists parodied Christian rites to invoke the Devil; there seemed to be a parallel here.

Telontas sighed. "Her voice was coarse and harsh, not her voice at all. She spoke gibberish, and I knew that some evil spirit without proper speech had taken possession of her. The king kept pressing us to question her, and at last she gave a great cry and burst out of the sacred enclosure. Then she collapsed, tearing down the curtains as she fell. I could see that the holy tripod had been knocked down, inside the enclosure. The Pythia never regained consciousness. She died this morning." The old priest was silent for a moment. Then he said quietly but bitterly, "The king said nothing but that he would try again when the god was in a better mood; he may come here today."

"He had better not," I said, moved by an impulse I could not analyze. "Apollo is not lightly mocked."

The old priest looked earnestly into my face and seemed to like what he found there. His back straightened, and his voice was calmer as he said, "You will be a true Pythia. I had my worries about the last girl even before all this happened. The god will truly speak through you, and all will be well again. I think that there is no need to tell you very much of the Pythia's duties; you are one to whom the god will speak clearly. A few simple things, though, you need to know."

He led me to the little hut and opened the curtain. The space inside was barely enough to stand up in and move around a little. In the center of the enclosure was a tripod made of three poles tied together near their upper ends. In the small space made by the protruding short upper ends of the poles was a shallow bowl holding black and white beans. The poles raised the bowl to about waist height. Near the tripod was a small footstool.

"Most questions asked of the god can be answered yes or no," said Telontas. " 'Is it better that I marry?' 'Is it better that our city make peace rather than go to war?' 'Is it better that we keep our old customs rather than change the laws?' If the god does not give you a verbal answer, put your hand in the bowl and choose a bean;

the god will guide your hand. If the bean is white, tell me, 'It is better.' If it is black, tell me, 'It is not better.' "

Telontas went on more slowly and solemnly. "At times the god will put words in your mind; simply tell them to me, and I will put them in words the inquirer can understand or, if there is need to be prudent, in more ambiguous words. But once in a great while, with a Pythia of unusual talent, the god may do more than put words in her mind; he may open his mind to her, let her see things as he sees them. I can tell you little of this. I have never experienced it. A few times I have acted as interpreter, as prophet, for a Pythia in this state. I did not know whether to envy or to pity her. But even to listen to the words she spoke was one of the strangest experiences in my long life."

He was silent for a little while, then said gently, "Do not let me frighten you, child; it is not likely that anything of this sort will happen to you. If it does, do not concern yourself too much about the inquiry. Tell me what you can, but most of all, lay yourself open to the gift of the god. It is a gift, and a great one. But perhaps I have said too much; we do not even know whether the god will be present today."

I had thought that the growing sense of unease I was feeling was due to the strange words of the old priest, but now I realized that what I was feeling came from without, not within. There was the tingling feeling I had felt before when the Path was open, and mingling and warring with that sensation was another, the prickling, itching sensation I had felt just before I reentered the Path after Apollo had killed the Pythian serpent. "We don't need to worry about whether the god will come," I said grimly. "Something will be here soon, and I hope that it is only Apollo."

The old priest shot me a startled glance. "I will have the goat brought in," he said. "If the omen is good, we will begin. Some say the old Powers from Below contend with the god for the mastery of this shrine, but I do not think that the god would let them give his sign. Go into the holy place, child, and gather your strength. As well as hold the lots, the bowl in the tripod can be used as a seat; it is an old custom, and not disrespectful to the god. I am told by the Pythias that it is not uncomfortable." With a nervous smile the old priest bustled out to begin the rituals.

I walked down the flight of steps to the little hut. At first I couldn't figure out what it was made of. Then I realized that the curious translucent covering of the hut was made of thousands of feathers, stuck together with wax. I went inside and pulled the curtain closed. From the inside the hut was a bright little cubicle. The walls of the room outside did not go all the way to the ceiling, and the room was lit by sunlight filtering in from outside. The translucent covering of the hut seemed to make it lighter inside than it was in the room outside.

I mounted the little footstool and seated myself in the shallow bowl. As Telontas had said, it was quite comfortable, and the tripod was heavy enough to be stable. Eventually the lack of a back and the slight pressure of the rim of the bowl on the backs of my thighs might make me uncomfortable, but for the moment I was fine. I put my hand down at my side and felt the beans beneath my fingers; it would be easy to pick one up without looking at it if I used that method. But somehow I felt I would not. Outside the little hut I heard movements and the bleating of a goat. There were a few mysterious clanks and rustles. Then I heard Telontas say: "The omen is favorable. Let the first inquirers enter."

I was tempted to get down from the tripod and peek out through the curtain, but I thought that this might be un-Pythia-like behavior. There were sounds of a small group of people entering the room and seating themselves on the benches, and I thought of high school plays where the cast waited behind the curtain as the auditorium filled. There were the same sounds of shuffling, coughing, a little murmured conversation. Telontas soon put an end to that; I heard his voice say, "Let your behavior be seemly and your thoughts fixed only on the god."

I supposed that applied to me too. I tried to relax as I sat on the tripod and to make my mind a blank, as I had when I had waited near the Tholos. I was a little startled when I heard a voice quite close to me; the inquirer must have been standing fairly near the curtain, in the little flat area at the foot of the stairs in front of the hut. It was a man's voice, and it sounded old. It spoke in classical Greek, which I understood about as well as the Greek of my own day. Whatever power had given me the ability to understand the languages of the past times I came to through the Path seemed simply to make me hear the main language I would need as if it were English; it did not give me the ability to understand other languages unless I already knew them. The man was asking something about marriage. "Is it better that I marry . . ." But that was all that I could understand.

I was beginning to panic; how could I answer questions that I could not understand? But then I heard Telontas speaking; he must have been standing near the inquirer. "Myron of Levadia wishes to know if it is better that he marry the young girl whose family has offered her to him or the older woman with a better dowry." I drew in breath to answer; if it were up to me, that old man would take someone close to his own age.

But suddenly I realized it was not up to me; this was not play-acting. I had offered myself as the Pythia, and I *was* the Pythia. Pictures flooded into my mind: Myron's face, the face of a well-to-do peasant, perhaps a little slow, a little greedy, but not unkind. Then a sour-faced older woman sneering at him because of the large dowry she had brought, a cold, unhappy house, meals eaten in silence. Now another face, the cheerful, sensible face of a young peasant girl with no romantic illusions, beaming at her wedding, pleased to have a well-off, not too demanding husband. I saw her pregnant, with Myron, proud and a little surprised, fussing over her. I saw the couple beaming over a cradle and later a sturdy little boy riding on the shoulders of his gray-bearded father. Words came to my lips. "It is better that he marry Dorcas and forget Maralia's dowry."

I heard Telontas translating and a babble of thanks from Myron; the decision evidently pleased him. I slumped on the tripod, shaken. The knowledge was already fading from my mind, but while I had seen those pictures, I had briefly known those people, known their lives in a way that was deep and intimate.

The next inquiry was easier: a pompous, official voice with a long question and Telontas giving me the gist of it in two sentences. "He represents the officials of a town on the plain. They want to know whether to drain the swamp next to the town and make it into farmland." This time I waited for the pictures to come into my mind; I saw men in armor creeping through the tall stalks of grain, an assault on the town, rape and pillage. Somehow I knew that the fields the invaders had crept through were the drained swamps, which had protected the town on that side from just such an assault. "It is better not to drain the swamp," I said.

This time the reply seemed unwelcome; the pompous voice grumbled and protested until Telontas cut it off with a sharp reprimand. I wondered if the officials of the town would be wise enough to take the god's advice. I was breathing a little faster; the scenes I had glimpsed of the sack of the town had been horribly real and concrete.

The next voice I thought at first was a woman's, but I remembered that no woman but myself was allowed in this part of the Temple. Again the question was a long one, and the translation by Telontas was much shorter. "It is the priest of Apollo from a little village in Arcadia. The women there are leaving their homes at night to follow the new god, Dionysos. He would like to stamp out this cult and asks the approval of Apollo."

I knew what my answer would be, but I was willing to wait and see what pictures would come to my mind; my first reactions had been wrong before. But no pictures came; Apollo was sulking, I thought with a little smile.

Should I choose a bean from the tripod and let that decide? No, I decided; if Apollo wouldn't give me any guidance, he'd have to take the consequences of leaving me on my own. "Tell him to honor Dionysos and leave those who wish to worship him free to do so," I said. "There is no need for Apollo and Dionysos to quarrel."

This time I could understand the reaction of the inquirer; the priest of Apollo had made his inquiry in Greek, but now he remonstrated with Telontas in the older language. "Lord Telontas, surely this is not the policy of the Temple? How can I tell the elders this? These women are getting out of hand. . . ."

The voice of Telontas was troubled, but he said firmly enough, "The Pythia has spoken, my brother. It is not for you or me to dictate to the Olympians." The other priest kept on protesting, but from the sound of their footsteps, Telontas was leading him back up the stairs. "There are other inquirers, Brother," he was saying. "You have had your answer."

Now one inquirer followed another until the pictures that came into my mind began to blend and merge, and I began to see first the immediate future and then more dimly the remote future all in one. Some events stood like rocks amid the shifting sea of other events, which changed and re-formed even as I watched them. There was not one future, but many, yet all these futures had some events in common, and it was of these that I could speak with confidence. Sometimes my answers had to be ambiguous because the events themselves were still unsettled.

As the future laid itself out before me, I began to see the past behind me. A scrap of something I had read about the Delphic oracle floated to the surface of my mind: "Under the influence of the god the Pythia saw all time and space as one." I did not do quite that; perhaps no merely human mind could. But I came closer to it than I would have believed possible.

Now I realized that it was not only my own voice I could hear giving decisions, not only Telontas I could hear interpreting my words. I was tuning in to—almost becoming one with—other Pythias, past and future. I seemed to speak their words and think their thoughts. I could feel age or sickness or fear in some of them, but in others I felt a serene confidence, a strength from which I drew strength. My mind could not hold all those oracles or all those Pythias, any more than they could hold all of the past and future, but some vivid scenes stayed in my mind, even as the total vision faded.

In one scene a young man stood before me, and I could see him in my mind sitting and listening intently while an older man with an ugly, clever, snub-nosed face challenged and questioned and talked of ultimate things with a little circle of friends. Now young Chaerephon stood before the oracle to vindicate his faith in his friend. "Is anyone wiser than my teacher, Socrates?" he asked confidently.

And even as I, the Pythia of that day, gave the answer "No one is wiser than Socrates," I could see those words echoing down the life of Socrates, who refused to accept the title of wise man and went on questioning, questioning, to see what the god at Delphi could possibly have meant. I saw him standing trial at Athens, brought down by the envy of those whose pretensions to wisdom he had deflated, saying the words that his friend Plato had later written down. "What in the world did the god mean? . . . for I know in my heart that I am not wise in anything. . . . I had to go on trying to find out what the oracle meant, questioning all those who had the reputation of wisdom. . . . I found that I was wiser than they because I knew I did not know, and they believed that they did. . . . I asked myself on behalf of the oracle whether I should prefer to be as they were. . . . I answered myself and the oracle that it was best to be as I am."

In another scene, which lingered in my mind from the experience of some long-ago Pythia, it was a delegation, serious, worried men from Athens asking if their city had any chance against the invaders from Persia. I could feel the Pythia of that day giving way to terror as she saw, in future after future, Athens leveled to the ground, its citizens killed or enslaved, the holy buildings on the Acropolis going up in flames. I was the Pythia, feeling her terror as she cried out, "Unhappy man, why are you wasting time? Flee from your homes, from the hills of your town. Your heads are not safe on your bodies, nor your toes and fingers on your limbs; all will be destroyed. Everything falls in ruins before the god of war in his chariot from the east. He will destroy many strongholds, not just yours. The temples of the gods will go down in fire and blood. Leave my shrine, and prepare your heart for sorrow."

But even as I, the Pythia, cried out these words, I could see that the future changed, for the Athenian envoys did not panic at this terrible prophecy; their courage rose to meet disaster. "Give us a better oracle about our land," one cried, "or else we will never leave this shrine. We will remain here till we die."

Now I could see one avenue of hope shining down the future: Athenian ships fighting the Persian fleet—and winning! I spoke again. "When all the rest has fallen, the gods will give you a wooden wall which will save you and your children. Do not hope to win with infantry and cavalry; at some other time you can fight them on land. But the Holy Island of Salamis will see you destroy the enemy when the grain is sown or when it is gathered."

Even as I spoke, I could see that the envoys would interpret my riddle and trust to the wooden walls of their ships; I could see the Persian fleet go down at Salamis in the spring, and Greece saved for freedom. But as I spoke the oracle, I could feel something dark and old, tearing at my mind, trying to prevent the words that would lead to a Greek victory. There was a light in Athens that this Dark Power wanted to extinguish.

"Should I go to war with the Persians or make alliance with them?" came the harsh voice of an inquirer. The vision of all times in one faded from my mind; I was only myself, Alice Grant, slumping in fatigue on the holy tripod, while outside the enclosure, Telontas was translating the words. And tearing at me with a force that seemed irresistible was that Dark Power I had felt in the memory of that previous Pythia, battering at me, trying to force me to tell this king to ally himself with the Persians, to help the dark tyranny of the East put out the clear light of Greece!

# CHAPTER
# FOURTEEN

The pressure was so strong that I felt as if the words were trying to force themselves through my lips. "It is better to make peace." I clapped both hands over my mouth and tried frantically to call out with my whole mind and soul for help. It was not Apollo to whom I instinctively turned; I still felt the sting of his words about interference the last time I had seen him. My sharing in his mind, if that was what I had been doing while acting as the Pythia, was somehow impersonal; I had felt no sense of an individual personality. Yet, if not Apollo, whom could I call on? No ordinary human help would be of any use against this assault on my mind.

Two images came to my mind: the indomitable wildness of Dionysos and the serene strength of Athena. I tried to hold the images, to send out a call with every bit of my mind and heart. And a response came! I felt a flood of wild, reckless joy, an infusion of power from which the dark tide sullenly retreated. Again images of the future flooded into my mind, troops crossing a river the name of which I somehow knew, a battle that would be decisive. "King Croesos, if you cross the river Halys with your army, you will destroy a great empire," I heard myself saying.

And even as I said it, I could see the king in his arrogance hurling his troops against the Persians, never doubting that it would be their empire that would fall. Yet it was his own empire that he would destroy, and he would be led away captive, bitterly complaining, too late, of the ambiguity of the oracle. But though the Persians would win, it would be at some cost to themselves; they would be less powerful than if Croesos had become their ally. The delay in their plans, the lessening of their strength would be enough to make it possible for the Greeks later to resist them successfully.

The vision was fading from my mind, but I could see a little ahead in time how Croesos, before the war, would ask the oracle whether he should take any allies. The Pythia would tell him to ally himself with the greatest of the Greeks. Croesos, thinking only in terms of military power, would ally himself with the Spartans rather than the Athenians, giving Athens a breathing space to build up its power so that it could lead the eventually successful resistance to the Persian threat.

But for now Croesos seemed satisfied; I heard through the curtain the sounds of his departure and a quick murmur from Telontas: "Rest a little, my child; there will be no more inquirers till we have made our farewells to the king. He is pleased; he does not see that the god's words are double-edged."

I breathed deeply and tried to relax, shutting my eyes and letting my mind wander. Where had that sudden surge of power come from? It *felt* somehow like the power of Dionysos, but would he have any power here in Apollo's sanctuary? I heard a little chuckle and opened my eyes. The hut had vanished, and I sat on the tripod in a place which seemed to be like that where I had met Athena, except that the blank gray background seemed tinged with gold, as did the mists that curled in wisps around the feet of the tripod. Before me stood Dionysos, his eyes laughing.

I slid off the tripod and faced him. "It was you then," I said. Then, half-teasingly, I went on. "Apollo won't be pleased; he doesn't like interference." Dionysos grinned, and it was impossible not to grin back at him.

Before he could speak, a voice came from behind me. "You're quite right, I don't like interference, either by Dion or by you and my sister. This oracle is mine, and no one can take it from me, neither the Dark Powers nor the other Olympians." I turned and saw Apollo standing there, his face arrogant and stern.

As I would have guessed, that arrogance only aroused the spirit of mischief in Dionysos. "So you say, Brother," he drawled, "but the Dark Powers nearly wrested the oracle from you today, if this girl hadn't been an unknown quantity to them and if I hadn't helped her. As for another Olympian taking it from you . . ." Dionysos put out his hand and grasped the tripod as if to carry it off. "You might be surprised what I could do if I put my mind to it." The dark-haired young god smiled insolently at his golden-haired half brother.

"Stop it, both of you," came another voice, and I was not surprised to see Athena suddenly appear, standing between the two brothers. She gave me a little smile, then said sternly, "If we quarrel among ourselves, what chance have we of defeating our enemies and carrying out our trust? 'Pollo, you should know that this place has too much power for one of us to control, especially one of us younger Olympians. You made no objections to letting me have a shrine at your gates; let Dion have a place here too. It's foolish to despise Dion because his mother was a mortal; he has his own powers that will complement ours. And you should be thanking this girl for her courageous help, not growling at her."

"The oracle is mine," said Apollo, not arrogantly now but almost pleadingly.

Dion let go of the tripod and touched his brother lightly on the shoulder. "I don't covet your oracle, Brother," he said. "Or your temple either; I'm not fond of temples. All I ask is that you let your future Pythias do what our young friend here did today: put the authority of your oracle behind my followers, prevent them from being persecuted. In return I'll use my powers to keep your Pythias safe from attacks like the one today. Let some of my initiates accompany your priests in the sanctuary. They can be men if you insist; I have plenty of male followers. I can focus my power through them at need, as you focus yours through the Pythia."

Dionysos turned his brilliant eyes toward me and smiled. "Your temporary Pythia has seen my theater beside your temple, not in a vision but with her waking eyes," he said to Apollo. "And what else?" he asked me.

"A great stadium, for the Pythian games," I said. "They were second only to the Olympian games in importance."

Dionysos turned triumphantly to Apollo. "A stadium," he said. "Athletic competition instead of war: That's one of your plans for the greatness of this land, isn't it? I don't grudge you the games or the oracle; don't grudge me the theater, or the slopes of Parnassos for my maenads. You know I have a way with the Wild Ones; they, too, can guard your sanctuary."

Apollo looked at his half brother with narrowed eyes. "There is an object which is closely tied up with your powers—you know what I mean. Will you leave it there in my temple as a pledge of trust?"

Dionysos hesitated, then nodded slowly. "If this place is not safe, no place is," he said. "Yes, I will leave it there. I could hardly give you a better pledge of trust; you know that if wrongly used, it could become deadly to me."

Apollo smiled grimly. "Not only to you," he said. "Don't fear, Brother, it will be well guarded." He gave a short laugh. "I will tell my priests that it is the tombstone of Dionysos; let them make what they will of that." He turned to me. "It is a jest that means nothing to you, girl. It is better so; you know more than is altogether safe for a mortal already. In fact, your safety is a problem. I could guard you here; I am not sure that I can guard you on the Path. You have made enemies today."

I tried to meet that brilliant blue gaze. "Have I made an enemy of you?" I asked.

He smiled with a touch of genuine humor. "We can never be enemies, girl," he said. "But when you are a mother, see if you like being corrected by your children, even if they are right—all the more so if they are right. You have something of me in you, or you could not share my mind as the Pythia. Perhaps that is why we quarrel."

He frowned thoughtfully. "Yet there is something in you that responds to Dion too. I would not have said that one nature could respond to us both, but mortals can always surprise me, despite my knowledge. Perhaps that is why I distrust them. But for now," he went on in brisker tones, "it might be well to get you away from here before the Dark Powers can gather their forces to revenge themselves on you. I will tell my priests to send away the other inquirers—"

"No," cut in Athena. "I will take her place; it may fool our enemies for a little while. At the end of the day your priests can take me back to my temple. But even if the forces that were gathered here are fooled by that, the Dark Powers may still have the Path itself patrolled in some way."

"I don't understand," I said. "The first time I came into the past—my past, that is—I walked through that shadowy tunnel. And I did that on the way back, too, and something seemed to be trying to frighten or lure me into leaving the tunnel—"

"On the left side?" cut in Athena.

"Why, yes," I said, trying to remember each of the incidents. The sunlit landscape had been on the left, and so had the false Rock of Sibyl. "It did always seem to be on the left side."

"There are dangers for you in leaving that Path on either side," said Athena, "though they are rather different dangers. What you see as a tunnel, what we talk of as the Path is not just a single line. You are outside of all times and places, and if you knew how, you could travel to any of them. And not just times and places in your world; there are worlds which we speak of as higher or lower, lighter or darker than yours. If you left the Path on the left side, you would find yourself in the power of our enemies. If you left it on the right, you might be faced with things that you are not yet prepared to face—not evil things but things too great for you to bear."

"But it was only the first time that I came and went through that tunnel," I said. "When I met Dionysos, I came through darkness, somewhere near the Rock, and returned to Amphissa without seeming to go through any kind of path at all. Then, the next time, I swam under the water, and I think that when I came up things had changed—I was already there, wherever there or then was. And I seemed to go back to the Rock instantly. And this time I came from down near the Tholos, not very near the Rock at all. . . ."

Dionysos gave me a sympathetic smile. "It seems to make no sense, does it?" he said. "But there are reasons for everything that happened. 'Pollo told you that when you had been through the Path once, it would open more easily next time. The main Line of Power runs through the rock where you first entered the Path and through the rock higher up the slope that they eventually built into the base of 'Pollo's temple. But there are other Lines of Power nearby; which one you make contact with depends partly on your mind. When you came through and joined my thiasos, you came in darkness and you came with thoughts of rebellion against a man who tried to force his will on you. When you touched one of the Lines of Power, it brought you back in darkness to my thiasos on the slopes of Parnassos, where other women rebelled against men who would not let them be free."

"When you came this time," said Athena, "you came from my place and with the thought of me in your mind. The journey before this one is harder to explain, but there is a Line of Power that goes down to the sea, and 'Pollo used it when he drew the Cretans here to serve him. When you crossed that Line of Power, you were drawn back to the time it was most full of power. There are . . . crevices . . . in the fabric of your world, almost closed in your time. But once you have traveled the Path, it may open for you again if you touch a place where the barrier is weak."

"I see that, I think," I told her. "But why did I seem to come or go sometimes without going through any kind of transition? And why can't I do it again if the Path is dangerous?"

Athena hesitated and then spoke slowly. "It is hard to explain to one who is not an Olympian. We do not live in your world, and when we venture into it, we can carry only a certain amount of power from our own world. And this power must be used carefully so as not to upset certain balances. When he first called you, 'Pollo kept his use of power to a minimum by letting you walk the Path on your own; he needed all his power to fight the Pythia. You did walk the Path when you met Dion, though it looked different to you. He used his power to send you back; I do not know why he chose the place he did—"

Dionysos chuckled. "It was a person rather than a place I sent her to," he said. "Someone who was much in her mind was somewhere along that Line of Power." I suddenly realized that my words to Nikos had been true in a way; our meeting in Amphissa had been no coincidence. Dionysos grinned at me, and I could feel myself blushing a little as I smiled back.

Athena lifted her eyebrows and went on. "When 'Pollo sent you back to the Rock that time, he used his power directly. He was angry and perhaps not thinking too clearly," she added dryly. "Each time you are sent back by our power it is easy for you to slip back again in time; that is why you found it comparatively easy to contact me at the ruins of my temple. How can I explain it to you? Think of yourself and those who live in the same time as yourself as little figures on a high shelf. The others are well stuck down, but you've become unfastened. It's easy to jar you loose, so that you fall off the shelf and can be caught down below. But it's harder to get you back up again. Those below can't climb up with you and put you back carefully; their weight would break the shelf. They must throw you up and hope that you land safely."

She smiled a little grimly. "Not a reassuring comparison," she said, "but there is truth in it. If you were that little figure and were able to move, perhaps you'd prefer to clamber up yourself; in a sense, that's what you do when you walk the Path yourself. But now suppose that some enemy is trying to intercept that little figure which is you. If those who are trying to get you up on the shelf throw you there, the enemy may be able to snatch you in midair before you reach the shelf. If you're climbing up, you may be able to evade them."

"You're right," I said, "it's not very reassuring. You're saying that I'd be safer if I went through that misty tunnel and watched out for traps, as I did the first time, aren't you?"

"Yes," she said simply. "If we try to send you back with a direct use of our own power, that use of power will cause effects that will be visible to our enemies. If we simply open the Path for you and let you walk back on your own, very little power will be used, and you may escape our enemies' notice. Remember that to them you are very hard to see or predict."

"But suppose they do attack me in some way?" I protested. "If I can't go off the Path to right or left, how *can* I evade them?"

Athena nodded. "You are right. You must have a way of escaping them if you cannot get through without their noticing you. And there is only one way: You must be able to step off the Path at will and return at will." She turned to Apollo and Dionysos. "We must give her a source of power," she said. "There is no other way."

Apollo frowned. "Put such a thing into the hands of a mortal!" he protested. "What if it is lost or taken from her?"

Dionysos grinned. "You know that it cannot be taken from her; she must give it freely. Knowing what it means, she is not likely to be tricked into giving it up or be foolish enough to lose it. The only question is, what shall it be? It must be something from the Bright Land."

Athena nodded. "Nothing else will do," she said. "The only

question is what it shall be. We do not dare give her too great a thing or too small a thing. And it must draw her to the Path, not to places that she is not ready to go. Perhaps something of mine—"

"No," said Apollo. "This is something that I owe to her; she has been my Pythia. This should do." He lifted his hands to his head and took off the headband which confined his hair. Without it, his locks of hair fell more naturally, giving his face a less austere look. He held it out in his hands; it seemed to be a ribbon of white cloth with a simple design worked into it, like some sort of embroidery. "My mother wove this," he said quietly. "There is power in it, and perhaps a little wisdom. So long as it touches your skin, you will be on the Path if you are on a Line of Power; put it off, and you will return to the world you know. Even away from a Line of Power it has certain virtues, but do not use it lightly. And now, it is time for you to go."

"Thank you." I faltered, feeling both honored and dismayed. To be able to enter the Path or leave it at will seemed a tremendous gift, perhaps too tremendous. Before this I had been a puppet or a pawn; the gift made me a free agent. I looked around me and saw the walls of the little hut about me again, but I could still see the three Olympians, seemingly as solid and real as the tripod and footstool.

Athena spoke quietly but earnestly. "When you take the headband from 'Pollo, you will find yourself on the Path. I do not know what stratagem our enemies may have prepared, but I think it will be based on the calculation that we would send you back down the Path so quickly that you could not stop. If you go slowly and carefully, you can probably avoid it. Farewell, I hope we will meet again."

Dionysos gave me a warm smile. "I know we will meet again. Remember you are a maenad; nothing can defeat you," he said.

Apollo gave me a direct glance from those brilliant blue eyes. "I will not speak of thanks or rewards; the battle is not over. But the gift I am giving you is a pledge of things to come. Farewell," he said. As the band of white cloth passed from his hands to mine, I found myself alone in the familiar misty gray corridor, alone and beginning to be afraid.

I clutched the band of white tightly, then decided that I had better have my hands free. I started to put it around my head as Apollo had worn it, then wondered if my hair would prevent it from acting. Had he said it should contact my body or my flesh? My flesh, I was fairly sure, so I put it around my neck and tied it in a loose knot, putting the ends down my cleavage. A warm tingle seemed to come from the cloth, and my fear receded.

I began to walk down the misty tunnel, and with every step I took my confidence increased. Perhaps we had evaded the notice of the Dark Powers; perhaps I would have another peaceful passage to my own times. On and on I walked, with every step my hopes higher. Until at last my steps faltered and stopped, for across the Path—stretching from side to side and from top to bottom—was an impenetrable barrier of black, jagged boulders!

# CHAPTER FIFTEEN

I stared at the barrier, and the image in my mind was of myself hurtling through this Path, so rapidly that my transition to my own time would seem instantaneous, and smashing myself on those cruelly jagged rocks. Athena had been wise—I smiled a little at the obviousness of that—Athena, goddess of wisdom, had been wise to warn me. Indeed, this trap was one which assumed that I would be hurled down the Path by Olympian power and not that I would be walking it on my own. Was it my imagination, or did I smell a faint sickly sweet odor coming from those rocks in my way? Best to get away from this barrier as fast as I could. But where?

I hesitated, my hand touching Apollo's headband where it lay around my neck. Surely the thickness of these rocks must be a thickness in *time*, since by walking along this path, I traveled through time. So if I left the Path and waited awhile before reentering it, I might simply live through the time covered by those evil-looking rocks. But how long should I wait? The thought of reentering the Path and finding myself trapped in the midst of those rocks made me shudder. Well, no need to decide that now; I wanted to get away from those black, brooding stones. I pulled the ribbon out so that it lay over my shoulders outside my shirt. Since I had gone to the Tholos late in the evening, I was wearing a polo shirt under a nylon jacket. I tucked the headband under the collar, like a man's tie, and zipped up the jacket over it. Then I took my hand off the strip of cloth.

Instantly I was standing on the slope between the Temple site and the Rock of Sibyl. Around me were ruins; whatever time I was in was after the Temple had been abandoned. But that could be

anytime from about the fourth century A.D. up to the twentieth.
I looked around me for clues.

I certainly wasn't in my own time or anywhere very near it. The
ruins looked completely abandoned; weeds grew high around the
Rock of Sibyl and even in the cracks between the stones of the
paved walkway that passed below it. I decided to go uphill; I wasn't
ready yet to meet people, as I might if I went down toward the
village. The village! But surely for a long time after the decline of
the Temple there had been a village on this very site; the French
archaeologists who had excavated Delphi had paid large sums to
buy up the village land and move its inhabitants to the place where
the village stood in modern time. So I must be either in the era
before the village was built over the ruins of the Temple or in the
era after it had been excavated. But had there ever been a time after
excavation when the site was in such terrible shape?

For as I climbed the hill, I saw that there were weeds everywhere,
even small bushes and trees growing among the stones of the Temple. The seats of the theater were half buried in loose dirt and mud
that looked as if it had washed down from the slopes above in some
torrential rain. Only one column of the Temple was standing,
instead of the several columns which had been reerected in the
Temple as it was in my time. The scattered drums of the other
columns were tangled in weeds and undergrowth.

As I climbed higher, I had a small fright: A rock moved under
my feet and ambled away up the slope on stubby legs. After a heart-
stopping moment I realized it was one of the tortoises I had occasionally glimpsed on the higher slopes of the site when I had
explored it in my own time. The fact that these shy creatures were
wandering the area near the Temple and theater said a great deal
about the extent to which the site had been left desolate. I realized
that the only sounds I had heard since I left the Path had been
birdsongs and the sound of the wind in the overgrown trees. Was
I going to be a sort of Robinson Crusoe, marooned in a completely
deserted shrine?

Then two things brought me out of that dream with a bump. I
found my way blocked by a very ugly, very modern coil of barbed
wire, and from the road below the site I heard the unmistakable
snarl of a powerful automobile, accelerating around the turn from

the village. I was in the twentieth century, then, or at least the late nineteenth. Or had I overshot my own time and arrived after some catastrophe had led to the abandonment of the site? I hoped I could catch a glimpse of the car; would it be some primitive motorcar from the time soon after the site had been excavated or some supermodern contraption from a time after my own?

It was neither. As I made my way cautiously down the slope, using every patch of cover, the car came in sight, parked on the road about where the tour buses parked in modern times. It was a boxy, powerful-looking Mercedes, black and sleek, with a look of the thirties or early forties. Small red flags with a white circle at the center and some kind of black insignia in the circle flew from its front fenders. Already parked in the same area were two armored troop carriers, camouflage-painted, with black crosses on their sides. Men in black uniforms, along with some in civilian clothing, were getting out of the Mercedes. Standing at attention around them were men in field gray uniforms and helmets of a shape familiar from old war movies. A breeze caught one of the flags on the fender of the Mercedes and blew it straight out. The insignia in the center was a swastika!

Forgetting the need of concealment, I rose to my feet to stare. A harsh voice sounded behind me: *"Halt! Kommen Sie hier!"* I spun around to see a helmeted figure in a gray uniform on the path below me, pointing a rifle at me. Not very near, and a soldier uncle had told me that most soldiers couldn't hit a barn at twenty paces. I decided to chance it and run for cover; the last thing I needed now was to be captured by the German army that had occupied Greece during World War II! A shot sounded behind me as I ran, and I dived for a nearby bush.

As if the shot were a signal, the crack of rifles sounded from the slopes above. I twisted around and saw with mingled horror and relief the black- and gray-clad figures crumpling to the ground. One German soldier had almost reached the machine gun mounted on one of the personnel carriers before several shots tore into him, leaving him sprawled on the ground, almost touching the treads of the carrier.

I huddled in my bush, trying to control my harsh breathing, hoping against hope that I could pass unnoticed in the general carnage. But then I heard footsteps and saw scuffed dusty boots and baggy trousers through a gap in my concealing bush. Whoever was wearing boots and trousers stopped near my bush, and I heard a voice say in Greek, *"Exo."* That meant "out." He was telling me to come out of the bush.

When I saw the man's face, I had a shock even greater than any of those which had come before. Mustachioed, grime-stained, drawn with weariness and hard with determination, it was nevertheless a face I knew. "Niko!" I gasped. "What are *you* doing here?"

The man's face showed astonishment but no recognition. He hesitated, then said slowly and stumblingly, "I am no Nikos. Manos Petrides is my name. You are English? What you are doing here?"

Petrides! This man wasn't Nikos then, but he must be some relation. All I could do was hope that he had the intelligence and flexibility of the Petrides I knew. "I'm an American," I said. "You looked like a good friend of mine named Nikos, but I see now that you're not."

He looked at me with narrowed eyes. "You are American?" he said slowly. "With a 'good friend' who is a Greek, Nikos. How come you here?"

"I'm a student," I said. "I was running from the Germans. I got trapped here—"

He looked at me suspiciously. "There are such," he said slowly. "I have hear—heard. When your country came into the war, no more neutral, the Germans intern them. Some escape. Perhaps you are what you say; perhaps not. But now we must run. Other Germans will hear shots and come." He glowered at me, stroking his moustache, then said reluctantly, "Better you come with me alone. Some of our men Communists, don't like Americans. Some like young girls too much. Safer alone."

"Okay," I said. "I mean—*endaxi* and *efkharisto polee Kyrie Petride.*"

He gave me a little smile that reminded me of Nikos. "You speak some Greek. Good." A thought seemed to strike him, and he looked at me appraisingly. "You speak also any German?" he asked.

"Not very much," I said.

His eyes searched my face. "You want to help Greece?" he said. "Help fight Germans?"

"Yes, if I can," I said as steadily as I could, trying not to think of the sprawled bodies near the cars below.

"Maybe there is a way," he said shortly. "Come." He gestured up the slope, and we started climbing up the same trail I had come down.

He turned and led the way up the slope at a pace I could just barely follow. When we reached the barbed wire, which seemed to surround the main part of the site, we skirted it for a while; then we stopped, and Manos picked up a forked stick. He used this to push aside the coil of barbed wire, which had been cut in an inconspicuous place near the ground. After we had passed through the gap thus made, he pushed the coil back and kicked some gravel over the cut. "After some while we can come back," he said. "Not soon. Many Germans here for a while."

With a hollow feeling in my stomach I realized he was right. The Germans would probably swarm over the site, looking for clues to the guerrillas who had shot their men. It might be a long time before it was safe for me to get to the Rock and try to get back to my own time. Of all the times in the history of Greece for me to be trapped, this must be one of the worst. And of course, that must be one reason the barrier on the Path had been placed where it was; if I did not destroy myself by smashing into the barrier, the Dark Powers wanted me to be in a situation where it would be physically dangerous to get into the site. For that purpose the German occupation was probably better than other stormy eras in Greece's history, for in most of them the site of the shrine was simply neglected or forgotten.

After passing the barbed wire, Manos Petrides had begun angling up the slope in the direction of the village. I realized that we were heading toward the side entrance, which had always been padlocked during my stay at Delphi. When we reached the place where I thought the gate should be, though, there was no sign of fence or gate; we came out onto a dirt road and followed it until we reached the first straggling houses in the upper part of the village. There were fewer houses than in my time, and they were far poorer-looking. That was partly the war, I guessed, but partly the fact that Greece in the 1980s was more prosperous than it had been for most of its modern history.

Certainly the house to which Manos had led me was one that would look out of place in the bustling, prosperous Delphi of my time. It was a small house, the crumbling walls of which had not been whitewashed in a long time. Its roof was patched with rusty pieces of tin, and a single bedraggled chicken scratched in a little enclosure made of thorny branches. Manos knocked on a weathered, unpainted door, and it was opened by a little old woman in black. She smiled broadly when she saw Manos, revealing crooked, discolored teeth.

I got the gist of the hurried conversation in Greek between them; he was asking her to hide me from the Germans, and she was telling him yes, of course, she would, not to worry. Manos turned to me and said in English, "Thea Sophia keeps you safe for now. I am back so soon as I can. Now is necessary I go before Germans come." He set off up the hill, and I turned to the old lady, who drew me further into the house with a cheerful cackle of laughter and made me sit down on a low chair. Then she bustled off into the only other room in the house.

In a few minutes she was back with an armful of black garments, probably her own spare clothing, perhaps her good clothing. Her gestures made it obvious that she wanted me to undress and put the clothing on, but I shook my head and began to put the heavy skirt on over my jeans. She cackled gleefully and nodded. My jeans seemed to amuse her, but she seemed a little envious of my stout hiking boots; her own were old and cracked. She stroked the silky material of my nylon jacket wonderingly, and I realized that nylon garments were still in the future for the people of this time.

With a good deal of help from her I managed to dress myself pretty much as she was dressed. My own garments under hers made me reasonably bulky and shapeless. She tied a black kerchief like her own around my head, then went into the next room and came back with an ancient looking pair of scissors, which she handled with evident pride. She reached under her own headdress and pulled out the end of her braided hair. With a quick snip of the scissors she cut off a good couple of inches of her braid. She formed it into a lock of hair and slipped it under the kerchief at my forehead, where she fastened it to my own hair with an old-fashioned hairpin.

Then she did a little pantomime. She strutted up to an imaginary door and knocked on it arrogantly, then peered around suspiciously, holding an imaginary rifle at the ready. Then she pointed to me, bent over, wrinkled her already wrinkled face even more by squinting and pursing her lips and put on a dull, imbecilic look. I got the idea and tried to imitate her, making myself into a hunched, half-witted old woman. She cackled again and clapped her hands. *"Yiayia,"* she said, *"Germanee then tha koitazoun."* A *yiayia* was a grandmother or old lady, I remembered. *Germanee* was obvious enough, and the rest meant "they won't look." So if I played a dim-witted old woman, the Germans wouldn't even look at me, she was saying. I hoped that she was right and hoped even more that we wouldn't have to put my disguise to the test.

But in that I was overly optimistic. The old woman had made us some herb tea from a handful of dried leaves probably gathered on the mountain and had discovered from my attempts to thank her that I spoke some Greek. She was just beginning to put me through a catechism that made Kyria Amalia's probing questions seem only mildly curious when a heavy hammering came on the door. The old woman hobbled over to open it, appearing to grow more feeble and ancient with each step, and I tried to imitate her by sinking myself into the part of a dim-witted old woman. But when the door was rudely shoved open as soon as she had unlatched it, I almost dropped out of character from astonishment.

The German soldier who pushed arrogantly into the room was hardly more than a boy, thirteen or fourteen at most, and his cheap coarse-fibered uniform was too large for him. His face was thin and pale, and underneath his bluster was fear, for his knuckles were white from grasping his heavy rifle too hard. He hardly cast a glance at me; his eyes were darting about the room, looking for anywhere an armed man might be hiding. He went into the adjoining room with a rush, poking his rifle out ahead of him, but was back in a moment; the house was too bare to offer any concealment.

He did spare me a glance then, but I crouched down, letting the hank of white hair hang over my eyes, and his eyes passed contemptuously on. In a cracked bowl on the table was a single egg, and he seized it and furtively thrust it into one of his inner pockets, looking defiantly at Thea Sophia, who merely gave a kind of protesting whimper. Then he stamped out of the little house.

As soon as he was gone, Thea Sophia straightened up and cackled with laughter. *"To avgo etan paleo,"* she said, holding her nose to indicate that the egg had been *very* old. She put her ear to the door, then opened it a crack and peered out. When she was sure that the Germans were gone, she spit after them and then came back into the room and produced several eggs from where they had been hidden, in a niche behind a little picture of the Virgin Mary. With the help of some small onionlike tubers, which she had probably foraged in the neighborhood, she produced a quite creditable omelet. This, with a small piece of hard bread and more tea sweetened with honey, was our evening meal.

I managed to ask her whether the eggs all came from the dispirited-looking chicken outside. She laughed and shook her head; with the help of more pantomime she told me that her other chickens were hidden well away from the house. I began to see why Manos Petrides had brought me to the wily old woman; she was evidently very much a survivor and was managing to live adequately, if not well, despite the war and the Germans.

It was getting dark, and she lit a little lamp consisting of a wick in a small dish of oil—the kind of lamp that had been used in Greece for centuries. I had seen only one bed, a narrow mattress on a frame which lifted it a little off the floor. Knowing Greek hospitality, I was sure she would try to make me take it, and I was just trying to frame the words to insist that I could easily sleep on the floor when there was a scratching on the door which suddenly reminded me of my awakening on a morning that was centuries past and yet "this morning" also.

Thea Sophia darted over to the door and opened the latch. Manos Petrides slipped in quickly and silently. When he saw my disguise, he grinned in a way that for a heart-tearing moment reminded me of Nikos. "Very good to fool the Germans," he said in a low voice. "But you must put on again your *pantalones*. Before it is light, we must be high up the mountain. Not even here is safe now. One man is caught with a rifle in Arachova; already the Germans have burn five houses there, shoot ten people."

# CHAPTER SIXTEEN

Thea Sophia didn't like the idea of my leaving the house at that time of night with Manos; I wasn't sure whether her concern was for my safety, my chastity, or merely my night's sleep. At last she grumblingly let me go, with a quick fierce hug and a mumble that might have been a blessing. Manos Petrides led the way up the hill with his long, tireless stride, and soon my legs were aching from the effort to keep up. I was glad when he stopped in the shadow of a little patch of bushes to look back down at the town, which was almost all visible from that point in the light of the newly risen quarter moon.

The setting of the town was what it had been for centuries and would be in my time, but the town itself was almost unrecognizable. The row of hotels that was cantilevered over the edge of the valley in my day had not yet been built. There was only one building that looked like a hotel, a big, square old building with windows shuttered or boarded up. There were almost no lights in the town, and no traffic moved in the streets. I thought of the night that Nikos had driven me from Amphissa and had not been able to stop because of the traffic. I looked at Manos gazing down silently at the town and asked, "Are you from Delphi, Kyrie Petride?"

He nodded and replied almost in the same words Nikos had used: "Our olive trees are down in the valley, but this is our village. Many people still call it Kastri, the name from before the Frenchmen moved us from over the ruins." He spoke as if it had happened a short time ago, though it must have been more than a century. He went on slowly, "Some say Delphi is a pagan name, from bad old times when they worship devils here. The mother of my father was used to say our family came down from priests of Apollo. Perhaps true, perhaps no. But I am proud to say I am man of Delphi."

He turned and led the way up the slope again. It was nearly dawn when we finally arrived at our destination, a cave in a rocky cliff high up the slopes of Parnassos. I was nearly asleep on my feet from the long night hike and collapsed onto a pile of sheepskins without taking much of a look at my surroundings.

When I awoke, I could see light coming from the entrance of the cave, which was screened with burlap sacking. I got up, feeling unkempt and a little groggy, and stumbled over to the sacking curtain. Peeking through, I saw that it was early evening. A small smokeless fire burned outside the cave, and a gray-bearded shepherd was sitting beside it. When I emerged from the cave, he rose to his feet with grave courtesy. He wore the traditional shepherd's clothing, which had changed very little in the past few centuries, but cradled in one arm was a rifle that looked quite new and very deadly.

The old shepherd nodded and smiled. After laying aside his rifle carefully, he dug a blackened pot from the embers and spooned out into a bowl some stew, which smelled delicious. I wondered what it was made of but firmly suppressed my speculations and wolfed it down, with the help of a horn spoon and a small piece of hearth bread the old man gave me. When I was finished, the shepherd gave me a tin mug of water, then with a grin pulled a little flask from his clothing and offered it to me. I took a cautious sip and tried to suppress a cough; it was brandy, old and smooth but very strong. I held the flask back with a polite *efkharisto*.

The old man chuckled. *"Apo Germanous,"* he said, pointing to the flask and to his rifle. "From the Germans," that meant. I doubted that they had given up either rifle or brandy without a struggle. I was just about to ask about washing up when the old man snatched up his rifle and stood listening, his hand raised for silence. Then I heard a whistle like a birdcall, and the shepherd relaxed and gave an answering whistle.

It was several minutes later before the people with whom the shepherd had exchanged signals arrived. They were Manos Petrides and a short dark girl in a black dress, carrying a bundle. Manos and the old shepherd shook hands, and the flask was offered to Manos, who took a deep drag on it while the girl eyed me with frank curiosity. When Manos had finished drinking, she said to him in English, "Yes, she is like the picture. It is worth trying."

Manos turned to me and said, "This is Elena. She was used to be maid at the Hotel Pythian Apollo at Delphi. Now she is maid in the house of the German general who commands this district. Our British allies they wish to ask questions of this German general—in England. It has been done before, to capture a high German officer and get him to British submarine off the coast, but this man is well guarded. We try to think of a plan—"

Elena cut in. "You understand I work in the German's house to get information for our men. So always I look for something. This general is a man like clockwork, always everything the same. Only one thing about him is human: On his table by his bed is a picture of a blond girl, young, in a white dress. On it is written in German, 'For my dear father from his little Rosalin.' I think and think about this picture, and then I make a plan."

"A crazy plan," said Manos, "but perhaps—"

"We have no choice," said Elena. "At no other time could we get to him. But in the evening he always walks in the garden. If he would go out of that garden out of the gate and into the little valley below, there is a place men could hide and take him. But for no ordinary thing would he go into that valley; he would call a soldier and send him."

"We thought of many things," said Manos, "even asking a girl to go into the valley naked—" He stopped, embarrassed.

"Pah," said Elena. "He would send a soldier to tell her to put on her clothes. He is that kind of man; when you work in the house, you know. But *I* thought if he saw a girl who looked like his daughter, calling for help. . . . Perhaps then he would forget to be careful and go himself to see. So my aunts came with me to clean, looked at the picture, and made a dress. But no girl we could find looked right in it. We have no blond girls, and the only wig we could find looked ridiculous!"

"When I saw you," said Manos, "I remembered this crazy plan. I asked if you would help us, and you said yes. But you did not

know then what the help was. Perhaps the general only points a
gun at you and says, 'Come here or I shoot.' Perhaps he sends
soldiers. I cannot promise that you would escape."

"I'm willing to face the danger," I said slowly. "But to use his
affection for his daughter to trap him seems—"

Elena snorted impatiently and started to speak, but Manos cut
in. "I am not proud to do this," he said, "but it is necessary. And
remember that this man gave or at least approved of the orders to
burn and kill in Arachova. They did not shoot children, but some
children in Arachova have no parents now."

"All right," I said, trying to keep my voice steady. "I'll do it."

"Then it must be now," said Elena. "Tonight I know he is at
home because I have his car." She giggled at my look of surprise.
"His car and his driver. Petros was a taxi driver; now he drives for
the Germans. They think he is a collaborator, but he is like me;
he works for the Germans to destroy them. Sometimes he can take
the car to run their errands—if only they knew what other errands
that German car does." She laughed harshly. "But now you must
try this dress," she said. "Come with me."

She led me into the cave and produced from her bundle a white
dress. When she shook it out, I saw in dismay that it seemed old-
fashioned even for the 1940s. "Elena," I said, "suppose the daughter
has grown up? The picture may be an old one. . . ."

She shrugged. "Perhaps and perhaps not," she said. "But to him,
I think, she may still be that young girl in the picture. And if he
stops to think, we are lost, anyway, because how could his daughter
be in Greece?" I gave up and slipped out of my jeans and jacket
and shirt. I saw Elena eyeing my very plain bra and panties with
a slightly shocked and rather covetous look. After years of war any
kind of decent underwear must be rare. I didn't have any idea of
what a Greek girl, or an American girl for that matter, would wear
in the way of underwear in the forties, but evidently what I was
wearing was less than she expected.

The dress fitted well enough. It was too short, but that added
to the schoolgirl air we were after. Elena shook her head at my
shoes. "They are not right, but we have none that will do. Stand
so the grass hides them. For now, put on again the silk jacket and

the trousers. But we must fix your hair. In the picture it is tied behind with a ribbon."

A shock went through me; I had nearly forgotten Apollo's headband! I reached into my shirt, which I had left inside out, and retrieved the band of cloth. "This should do," I said, and quickly tied my hair back with it, reflecting wryly that I probably looked a good deal like my namesake, the Alice of *Alice in Wonderland*. There was a faint tingling in my hands as I tied the ribbon, but nothing else happened; of course, I was a long way from the Lines of Power. But all the same, I made sure that the headband didn't touch my skin once it was tied.

"Before the war the American young ladies who came to Delphi did not dress so," said Elena as she watched me bunch the skirt of the dress and struggle back into my jeans.

"It's the latest fashion," I said. At that, it might be. Wasn't it during the forties that teenaged girls went around in jeans, men's shirts, and saddle shoes with bobby socks? Outside the cave I shook hands solemnly with the old shepherd and set off down the hill with Manos and Elena.

Luckily the road where the car was waiting was not too far down the hill. The dark-haired, nervous-looking driver bundled us quickly into the back seat of the boxy old limousine and told us to keep our heads down. As I felt the car sway around the sharp corners of the mountain road, its tires squealing, I was just as glad I couldn't look out.

After what seemed hours, we stopped in a little patch of trees, and Manos and I slipped out of the car. As the car drove off, Manos said in a low voice, "We have some little time to wait while Petros warns the men and Elena finds if the German general will walk in the garden. But I think he will. Always his habits are very regular. I do not know if it is better to get in position now or wait until we are sure."

"I think it would be better to get all set before he comes out into the garden," I said.

"If he does not come out, we may have a long wait there without to be able to move, but yet it is better to be there already," Manos agreed. "Come quietly as you can; the path is much overgrown."

We went down the road a little, into the field and through some bushes. A narrow, overgrown trail twisted through the bushes. Manos whispered, "In peacetimes a rich widow lives in this house; in the little valley are fruit trees, and the children find this way in. Since the German is here, we forbid the children to come because at some time we know it will be useful to come this way in secret."

Presently there were walls of rock on either side of us; we were going through a little ravine that was hardly more than a crack in the rocks. When we came out of this ravine into the little valley, I saw that the house sat on a low hill on one side of the valley. The hill on the other side of the valley was higher than that on the house side. The small valley thus made a sort of sheltered, private backyard for the house. In the light of the moon, which was now high in the sky, I could see the pattern made by the fruit trees on the floor of the valley.

"There are German guards on top of the hill, but they cannot see into the valley," Manos whispered. "We must make our way to the side of the hill opposite to the house." Very slowly and carefully we worked our way along the slope of the hill. We had to go higher up before we could get down to where we wanted to be, and I could see over the house to the road outside. It was clear why the general thought he was safe here; the guards on the hill above us could see anything coming from any direction except from the little hidden ravine we had come through.

At last we were settled in the place we wanted to be: a little patch of bushes almost opposite the house. You could easily have lobbed a baseball—or a grenade—over into the garden from here. When I stepped out in front of the bushes, the general could see me well, but not too well.

It was a long, cold wait. I slipped out of my jeans and laid them across my legs as I crouched in the bushes; I had my jacket over my shoulders, holding it closed with my hand in front. All I would have to do was throw aside these garments and step out of the bushes, and I would be onstage and in costume for our little drama. After a long wait we could see (because we were looking for them) the faint movements in the bushes as several men made their way into the valley from the hidden ravine and positioned themselves in the undergrowth on the floor of the valley.

At last Elena opened a window of the house and shook out a dustrag. Evidently this was the signal we were waiting for. Manos gripped my arm so hard it was painful and whispered, "He is home and will soon take his little promenade in the garden. Be ready."

But there was another long wait before a tall, stooped figure in a gray uniform came out the back door of the house and began to stroll up and down the little garden just behind the house. I slipped off my jacket, threw off my jeans, and stood up in front of the bushes while he was walking away from me. As he turned and was about to come back, I checked my hair, and my fingers touched Apollo's headband. I felt a little tingle go through me; perhaps whatever powers this piece of cloth had might help me now. I pulled the band around so the bow was resting on the back of my neck, held down by my hair. The tingling sensation went through my whole body.

Now the general had turned and started back; he was looking down at the ground. I waited until he was a little nearer, then called out, *"Vater, Vater, hilfe!"* His head came up in an incredulous snap; I could see his jaw drop. I stretched out my arms and called, *"Hilfe!"* again, hoping that I had remembered the right words for "father" and "help." I didn't dare say much more; a grammatical error or a mispronunciation could ruin the illusion.

He stood there gaping for a moment while I willed him to see me as his daughter, willed him not to think of the impossibility of her really being there, but simply to react by instinct and run to me. And he did! With a broken cry of "Rosalin" he ran down the path, through the garden gate and down into the valley that separated us. I didn't risk any more words but simply held out my hands pleadingly.

The valley was small; in a few strides he was into it; in a few more he was at the bushes where the Greek fighters waited. Dark forms rose up around the gray-clad figure of the general; something was thrown over his head, and he went down with hardly a sound. The low voice of Manos sounded in my ear: "Thanks to you we have got our German general. Now we shall see if we can get him and ourselves out from here alive!"

Whether it was euphoria because our fantastic gamble had succeeded or something to do with the headband, which was still touching my neck, I was filled with a serene confidence. "The guards haven't noticed a thing," I told Manos, "and they won't if we get him out the way we came, quickly and quietly." He looked at me strangely but nodded his head and led the way. The men holding the general were already carrying him toward the little ravine through which we had entered the valley.

Three men had the German officer, swathed in a heavy blanket, and were walking in a single file, carrying him on one shoulder as if he were a heavy log or girder. He did not seem to be struggling even when they stopped for a moment and shifted him to the other shoulder. I followed the three men, and Manos brought up the rear. Speed seemed to be more important to them now than caution, for they almost ran up the valley and pushed their way through the undergrowth in the ravine without much effort to conceal the traces of their passage.

When we arrived back at the little patch of trees where Petros, the driver, had dropped us, he was there again with the same car. There was a quick conference in Greek, too rapid for me to follow, and Manos turned to me with a troubled expression. "They want to drive him down to the coast in his own car. With Petros driving it will look very normal. But there are checkpoints, and they think it will keep away suspicion if you are also in the car, dressed as you are now. They are perhaps right, but if we are stopped—"

"I've come this far," I told him. "I may as well see it through." I watched with concern as they unwrapped the blanket around the general; if they had hit him too hard, all this effort would be wasted and I would feel like a murderer because I had lured him to his death. But he was alive and beginning to regain consciousness. They bundled him into the back, and Manos lay down on the floor in the space between the front and the back seats, where one of the other men covered him with a blanket. Manos was carrying a large, ugly-looking pistol; it was the first time I had seen him armed.

At a gesture from one of the men I sat on the back seat beside the general, and Petros got into the driver's seat and started the motor. The other men lifted their hands in farewell and melted back into the shadows as we moved off. Manos pushed aside the upper part of the blanket and looked up at us from his position on the floor. "General Kroenig," he said softly, "I know that you speak English, and I want you both to understand what I am saying. We are going now to the coast, where we will be met by a British submarine which has been summoned by that wireless transmitter you were never able to find. You are a prisoner of war, General; cooperate with us, help us get through the checkpoints without trouble, and you will be treated well. The war is over for you; if we are captured, my orders are to shoot you. The British want to question you, but they do not use the methods of your Gestapo; if you are wise, you will go quietly. This girl is not your daughter—"

"No," said the general quietly, "she is not my daughter. My daughter was killed in an air raid two days ago. She was the last of my family. My son was lost on the Russian front; my wife died early in the war. I am very weary, my Greek friend, and if it were only you and I, perhaps I would give the alarm at the checkpoint and cheat you of your triumph. But then this girl would die or fall into the hands of the Gestapo. As you say, they are not gentle. And though she is not my daughter, for a few moments there in the moonlight I thought she was; God knows what I thought. Knowing what would happen to her, I do not think I will cry out. So you win."

He turned to me and said, "You are a brave woman, Fräulein, to play this little charade to capture me. You are of the British service?"

I shook my head. "I'm an American, a tourist really. I got trapped here while I was traveling—"

"And the Greeks made use of you," he said with a touch of bitterness. "They are good at that. But I cannot blame them. War is not a game, and the only rule is to win how you can. I am not sorry that my duties are over. I have had to do things that will give me dreams to disturb my sleep while I live. And that may not be long."

"Even the worst things are forgotten in the end," I said, thinking of the German tourists who thronged Delphi in my own time and bought woven goods in Arachova, where houses had been burned, and people shot. "Your life isn't over, General," I went on. "You'll be safer interned in England than you would be here. And after the war there will be a new life for you, even a new family." I saw no pictures in my mind, as I had when I had acted as the Pythia, but I was sure that what I said was true.

The general shot me a startled glance. "So there is still a prophetess at Delphi, Fräulein? Well, perhaps you are right. Do you accompany me on my submarine voyage?" he asked.

"Yes, she will," said Manos. "It was in my mind when I asked her to do this. I do not know if she can get back to America in wartime, but at least her parents will know she is safe in England."

It was hard for me not to break out into hysterical laughter. I wasn't quite sure where in the war years we were. My parents were still teenagers in America. They hadn't even met yet. And if, with the best intentions in the world, I was shipped off to wartime England away from Delphi and the Rock, I might never get back to my own time. Since I had no background, no history that could be checked and confirmed, I would very likely find myself in some sort of internment camp if I did reach England. I said nothing but resolved to get away from this situation as soon as I could. But how?

The first test of the sincerity of the general's words came when we passed a German checkpoint as we neared the coast. The sentries snapped to attention when they saw the general in the back seat. The young officer who was with them, though plainly curious at what I was doing in the car, merely waved us by as the general nodded at him and gave him a small, constrained smile. I wasn't entirely reassured, though; we could probably have forced our way through the roadblock even if the general had tried to give the alarm. He might simply be waiting for a situation where he could be sure of more effective help.

When we reached the coast road and began to drive into Itea, I could almost feel the tension from Manos beneath the blanket at our feet. I saw why in a moment. At the point where the road entered the village, there was a barrier, and a small house had been taken over as a guardpost. A heavyset man with stripes on his sleeve seemed to be in charge, but he managed to delay us until an officer came out of the house, yawning and buckling his uniform belt. His uniform was black instead of gray, and his outwardly respectful bearing toward the general had a touch of insolence behind it.

There was a sharp exchange of words in German between the general and the black-clad officer. Without being able to understand a word, I was pretty sure that the objection was to me: as a woman; as a civilian; as a non-German. I wasn't sure which. Finally the general gave a direct order to the gray-clad NCO, who opened the barrier with a very unhappy expression on his face. The black-clad officer stood looking after us in impotent fury, his fists clenched at his sides.

As we moved off, Manos pushed aside the blanket and looked up at us. His face was beaded with sweat, and I realized how difficult it must have been for him, stifling under his blanket while the rapid German phrases passed over his head. "The general got us through," I told him.

"That is the kind of man," said the general bitterly, "who will lose us this war, the kind of man who made the Russians rise up against us when with a little cleverness, a little kindness they might have welcomed us to deliver them from Stalin." I remembered that he had lost a son in Russia and wondered if his bitterness was connected with that. "That was the man who gave the order to kill and burn in Arachova," the general went on, half to himself, "because one old man was found with an ancient gun."

"We will remember that," said Manos, his voice soft but deadly.

The general flushed, realizing perhaps that he had signed the black-clad officer's death warrant, and said angrily, "Your own hands are far from clean. Some of the men you shot down at the ruins were distinguished archaeologists from Berlin, concerned only with the damage that neglect might have done to the site."

"General," said Manos, "we Greeks love our heritage. When we besieged the Turks on the Acropolis, they were throwing down the columns to get lead for bullets from the lead pins which held the drums together. The Greek besiegers sent a message to them: 'Leave the columns alone; we will send you lead for bullets.' And they did! But we would let every stone of our heritage be cast down before we would give up our freedom."

"They were old men, scientists," said the general wearily. "They loved your heritage, too, in their way."

Manos was silent for a while, then said quietly, "I do not say that I am proud of what we did at the ruins, General, but I am not too much inclined to weep for your scientists. Too many of them tried to make Apollo an Aryan and despised the Greeks of today. *We* are not Aryans."

It was a strange debate, conducted in the big old military car as it swayed and bumped its way down a road which was potholed and broken-surfaced from the long years of wartime neglect, compounded by heavy military traffic. I could see the two men's faces only by the moonlight that came in the car windows; the dashboard lights and even the headlights were dimmed in accordance with blackout precautions.

Before they could continue their argument, the car slowed and turned, bouncing over ground even rougher than the road. As the car stopped, Manos rose to a crouch and waved us out of the car with his pistol. We stumbled out, stiff and bruised from our wild ride, and saw that we were on a rocky little beach, with the car leaning at a drunken angle where Petros had run it off the road. I suspected that he had resigned as a chauffeur for the Germans and that the car might not serve the Germans much longer either.

Petros was looking out to sea, with a heavy flashlight in his hand. He pointed it out at the waves, and I could see the light blink in an irregular pattern. From the shadowy sea there came a pinpoint of light flashing in some sort of code, and before long a small rubber boat, rowed by a man in dark clothing, came into shore. His voice was very English as he said, "That had better be bloody important cargo to risk the ship this close to the town."

"It is," said Manos. "A German general and a girl who helped us capture him. Take the girl first—"

"No," I said. "The general first, and quick."

"Whichever it is, get them in the dinghy, quickly," said the Englishman.

Looking at me unhappily, Manos pushed the general forward. He seated himself docilely enough in the little rubber boat and lifted his hand to us in farewell.

"Perhaps we will meet again to continue our discussion," he said to Manos, and then to me: *Auf Wiedersehen,* Fräulein; I look forward to our voyage together." Then the impatient Englishman had him out to sea.

"You should have gone first," said Manos. "For *him* they would be sure to come back, but for you—"

"If he had stayed, the whole thing would have been wasted," I said. "Don't you hear the cars on the road?" Powerful engines could be heard on the road from the direction of town; then came the screech of brakes as someone spotted our car. "I don't know about the rest of you," I said fiercely, "but I prefer the deep blue sea to the devils."

I threw off my white dress, grabbed my jacket, and kicked off my shoes, then headed for the shore in my underwear, trying to get the jacket on as I ran. As the ribbon, no longer partly held away from my neck by the collar of the dress, touched my neck, I felt a deep tingle go through my body. A hope that I had hardly dared acknowledge to myself grew stronger. We were just outside Itea on the shore road, just about where I had been swimming when I had my adventure with the Cretan ship. There was a Line of Power here; one of the Olympians had said so. If I could only swim out to where it touched the sea . . . I struggled into the jacket as I plunged into the sea and began to swim.

Behind me men were shouting, and I saw the beam of a powerful flashlight playing over the waves. I wondered if the two Greeks had gone into the water after me. Evidently the Germans thought they had, for more flashlights and what looked like a small spotlight continued to shine out from the shore. Then I heard the staccato bark of a machine gun from the beach, and I dived under the waves. Swimming was hard at first, then grew easier, and I felt that I had been under the water for a long time without taking a breath. That was what had happened the first time I had swum in these waters and found myself coming up from the water to see the Cretan ship. Perhaps I was actually on the Path now!

Then a chilling thought struck me. How could I be sure that I would come back to my own time? There must be some relation between distance walked or swum on the Path and the amount of time traversed. But without the Rock to serve as a sort of marker, how would I know if I had gone far enough or too far?

Then I remembered something Dionysos had said, about sending me to a person rather than a place or time. If I held very hard to the thought of Nikos, perhaps I would be drawn again to a place and time where he would be. I was totally disoriented now, not sure how long I had been swimming underwater or in what direction. My lungs began to feel uncomfortable suddenly, and I swam for the surface as strongly as I could.

I came up swimming for the shore, and at first I thought that I had not moved in time at all, for it was night and there were lights on the shore. Then I realized that they were not flashlights, but lights on some kind of emergency vehicle on the road that ran parallel to the shore. No one was on the beach, but there seemed to be a little crowd of people around the flashing light. I swam to the shore and picked my way up the beach, wishing that I had been able to keep my shoes or my jeans. I was just barely decent in the soaked nylon jacket, which was long enough to cover my pants, but my first impulse was to avoid the group of people and try to slip away in the darkness.

I might have done just that, but there was a fear in me that the flashing light was connected in some way to the reason I had been sent along the Path to just this place and time. I had been thinking of Nikos, but surely . . . I walked up to the light, trying not to let my imagination run away with me. But it was not just imagination. As I came nearer, I saw the small Japanese truck, terribly familiar, slewed off the road, and lying near it on the ground, his face pale and bloody, was Nikos!

# CHAPTER SEVENTEEN

I rushed over to Nikos and knelt beside him. For some reason the little crowd of people around the vehicle with the flashing light seemed to be ignoring him. There was another car over there, terribly smashed up, and they all seemed to be clustered around it. Nikos was breathing, thank heaven, but blood was oozing from a deep cut on his forehead in a way that sent a wave of panic through me. Some kind of pressure bandage was needed on that, I thought frantically. Nikos always carried a crisply pressed spare handkerchief in one of his back pockets, I remembered, and I managed to reach under his inert body and pull it out.

I pressed the folded handkerchief to the wound and held it, but I was afraid to press too hard; there might be other injuries to his head or neck. I needed a bandage to hold the handkerchief in place. I tore the headband away from my hair and carefully worked it under his head and used it to tie the handkerchief firmly over the wound. Then I knelt gazing into the face of Nikos, frantically wondering what else I could do.

An injured man shouldn't be moved any more than you can help—I knew that much. I looked around desperately for someone to help, and finally someone came over to me from the group around the smashed car. He was in the uniform of the *chorophylakes*, the "country police" who handled most police duties outside large cities. "Please, is there a doctor or an ambulance for my friend?" I asked in English, ready to try again in Greek if he didn't understand.

Luckily he spoke English. "Someone is coming from Amphissa; they will be here soon," he said. "The drunks in the other car, who

forced your friend off the road, are very badly hurt. I was doing
what I could for them. Some fool said the driver of the truck was
dead, but it looks as if for a change the innocent party came off
better than the drunken driver. He is also a foreigner, your friend?"

"No," I said, "he's a Greek. His name is Nikos Petrides; he lives
in Delphi."

"I know of the family. They are very much respected," said the
policeman. "Kyrios Nikos I do not know; he is usually in Athens."
He looked at my soaked nylon jacket and my bare legs perplexedly;
then his face cleared. "Ah, I see. You are having a moonlight swim,
and Kyrios Petrides is coming to meet you here when they run him
off the road. A great shock for you, miss, but I think your friend
will be all right. His color is better now, and look, he is opening
his eyes."

In fact, Nikos was not only opening his eyes but trying to sit
up. "Oh, Niko," I said, "you'd better lie quiet until a doctor can
look at you." I burst into tears and couldn't stop, though I told
myself it was ridiculous to be crying when Nikos seemed to be all
right.

"I feel fine, Aleesah," said Nikos. "Just a little shaken up. Don't
cry, my darling. I was looking for you, but this is a hell of a way
to find you. What happened?" The policeman cut in with an explanation in rapid Greek, while Nikos sat up and stretched out his
arms and legs cautiously.

"And the young lady tied up your head," concluded the policeman in English.

Nikos grinned and with the help of a hand from the policeman
got to his feet. "That was sweet of you, Aleesah," he said. "It
probably looked worse than it is; scalp wounds can bleed a lot. I
don't even have a headache. Let's take a look at the truck; I don't
suppose that it came off as well."

We walked over to the truck. I watched Nikos carefully, but he
certainly seemed to be walking and acting normally. When we
reached the truck, I saw that the windshield was shattered. Nikos
grimaced. "If I hit that with my head, no wonder it was bleeding,"
he said. He got some gloves from the glove compartment and started
breaking the glass out of the windshield to make an opening. "Stay
back, Aleesah," he said. "There's a lot of broken glass here." Even-

tually he got enough glass out of the windshield to give him a clear view and swept the pieces off the seat and floor.

"Say a prayer," he said, climbing into the driver's seat. The engine ground for a minute, then turned over. Very slowly and cautiously Nikos backed the truck back up onto the road, then drove it forward a little. He got out, leaving the engine running, and walked around the truck to inspect it. He took a tire iron from the cab and levered the twisted bumper out a little, then threw gloves and tire iron back in the car. "I was lucky," he said. "They were on the wrong side of the road, coming straight at me. I went off the road on the shoulder and managed to slow up quite a bit before I finally hit that rock. The bumper took a lot of impact, though that front fender suffered a little. Would you like a very slow ride back to Delphi?"

"Of course, Niko," I said, "but are you sure you ought to drive?"

"I'm fine," he said, "just wait a minute until I talk to the *chorophylax*. He seems to be a good fellow; he'll probably let me take care of the formalities tomorrow." I saw him talk briefly to the policeman and shake hands with him. Then he returned to the car, and we started out, driving slowly for Delphi.

A few miles down the road Nikos stopped the truck. "I'm a fool," he said. "You were swimming, and your clothes and things must be back at the beach. I'll turn around."

"Oh, Niko, please don't bother," I said. "It's only my shoes and jeans and shirt and a few odds and ends. I don't think I could even find them on the beach in the dark." That was very true since the beach I had left my clothing on was about forty years in the past. "Please drive straight home," I pleaded. "I really don't think that you should be driving at all after the bump on the head you got."

"Well, okay," said Nikos reluctantly. "I only hope some tourist does not pick up your things and carry them off. If that happens, we will get you new things from the compensation. The boys in that car come from a wealthy family, and their father will pay to avoid trouble. Was your purse or passport with your clothes?"

"No, thank heaven," I said. "I don't usually carry my passport in Delphi, and when I'm just out for a walk, I often just put a little money for emergencies in my pocket and leave my wallet at home."

He nodded. "That is safe enough in Delphi; if you say you are at Amalia's place, it is easy enough to check. When you go as far as Itea, it is perhaps safer to carry some identification." I didn't tell him that I had set out that evening—at least I hoped it was that evening—only for the Tholos on the outskirts of Delphi.

When we reached the hotel, Kyria Amalia was waiting up, ready to give me a scolding for another late night out. But when she saw the shattered windshield and the bandage on Nikos' head, she was distracted from scolding me and full of questions and exclamations. I managed to pry Nikos loose from her and send him off home, then got my key and went up to my room, with Kyria Amalia at my heels.

"And it is not decent to dress so," she was saying, "and if your clothing is lost, it is a punishment. Why always are you swimming, swimming at Itea and missing the buses and causing worry to Kyrios Petrides when he comes to visit you?"

Eventually I got rid of her and fell into bed. I didn't know whether to bless or curse her rattling tongue. Evidently Nikos had stopped by the hotel for a late visit, waited long enough to get worried, and then set out in search of me. Remembering that the time I was out overnight I had said I was swimming at Itea and missed the last bus, he had eventually driven there to look for me. I didn't know whether to be glad that he had found me or sorry because of the accident.

Not surprisingly, the next morning I overslept, but when I came down, still tired and a little grumpy, Kyria Amalia made me some fresh coffee and had saved some bread for me. After breakfast I went up and checked out my wardrobe gloomily. I had left behind me on the beach my shirt, jeans, and shoes and socks. The shirt wouldn't be hard to replace or do without, but the loss of a good pair of American jeans and a comfortable, well-broken-in pair of hiking shoes was a major disaster. I looked over my remaining traveler's checks gloomily, wondering if I should try to replace the missing things or just do without them.

Presently there was a tap at my door. It was Kyria Amalia to tell me that "a gentleman" had come to see me. She seemed excited and, for her, a little subdued. I was surprised to find that she ushered me to a little parlor that was usually her private sanctum.

She pushed me gently into the room and then went out, leaving me with my visitor. He was a gray-haired man, very dignified and erect, with a marked resemblance to Nikos. I wasn't surprised when he said, "Miss Grant, I am the father of Nikos Petrides. First I wish to thank you for the help you gave my son last night. There was much blood on the handkerchief, but the wound seemed to be closed entirely. It seems almost a miracle."

I suddenly remembered that I had tied up the wound with the headband Apollo had given me. Apollo's words came back to me: "Even away from a Line of Power it has certain virtues." Apollo was called the Healer as well as the Lord of Light; perhaps the power in his headband was responsible for the quick recovery of Nikos. But I also remembered Apollo's warning about letting the headband get out of my hands. "All I did was apply a simple bandage, Kyrie Petrides," I said. "It must have been a clean cut that closed up as they sometimes do. You . . . didn't throw away the ribbon I used, did you? It was a gift from a friend, and I wouldn't want to lose it."

"You will have to get it from Nikos," said Kyrios Petrides with a little smile. "His mother wanted to take it away and wash it, but Nikos said that he wanted to keep it. I saw him tucking it into his shirt this morning, close to his heart."

"That was sweet of him," I said, resolving to pry the headband away from Nikos the next time we met. "And it was wonderful of you to come and thank me."

"Perhaps it is not the only thing I have to thank you for," he said obscurely. "When Nikos had the accident," he went on, "you were in the sea outside Itea. That is right?"

"Why, yes," I said, wondering what he was driving at. "I was swimming there. I've done it before."

"There is a story connected with that place," said Kyrios Petrides, and I wondered if he meant the story of the Cretan ship and the dolphins. But he went on. "Many years ago, during the war, a German general was kidnapped by Greek *andartes*—you would say 'guerrillas.' They were helped by a young American girl. The German, General Kroenig, was put aboard a British submarine near the place you were swimming. But German pursuers caught up with the *andartes* and the young woman. They had no choice but to swim out to sea to try to get away. The Germans fired at them, and it was believed that the girl was hit and either killed outright or so weakened that she drowned. But her body never came to shore."

"What about the men?" I asked. An unsettling suspicion was growing in my mind as he spoke.

"They both escaped by swimming out to sea and, coming ashore later in darkness, evading the Germans. But except for a few pieces of clothing which the girl had left and the Germans took, there was never any trace of the girl. Some of the people who heard the story said that there had never been an American girl at all. General Kroenig's daughter had died a few days before this; some said that it was the ghost of his daughter who lured him away so that he would be safely interned in England and his life would be saved."

"That . . . doesn't seem very likely." I said.

"No, because why would a ghost pretend to be an American?" said Kyrios Petrides gravely. "But there was a much more popular explanation. Many said that the girl was a *gorgona*; in English I think you say 'mermaid,' do you not?" I nodded. "You understand that the fishermen tell many stories about how these mermaids come out of the sea and pretend to be ordinary women, to lure men to destruction. But no one was lured to destruction, and why would a good Greek *gorgona*, even if she wished to help our *andartes*, pretend to be a girl from America?"

"What do you think is the explanation?" I asked, trying to keep my voice steady.

"At times I think that the girl was just what she claimed to be: a tourist from America trapped by the war," he said. "But there were some things about her that were very puzzling. She appeared mysteriously on the ruins of Delphi. The *andartes* had a plan to dress up a girl as the daughter of the general to lure him where they could capture him; they used the American girl because she was fair-haired. But the general knew his daughter was dead. Nevertheless, he came toward where the girl stood, like a man who walks in his sleep. And he put up no resistance because he did not want the girl harmed. That seems strange."

"Perhaps he was just sick of the war," I said. "After all, his wife and son were dead too." His eyes narrowed, and I realized that he had not told me that; I had given myself away. "You're Manos Petrides, aren't you?" I said.

He nodded slowly, awe on his face. "Yes, I am Manos Petrides. Your name I never knew, until now. I am not surprised that you did not recognize me. But you have not changed at all. When Nikos told me the clothing you had left on the beach and what it was, I wondered. When I saw you, I was almost sure. Now I am altogether sure."

I thought of spinning some tale about an aunt or even my mother's being the mysterious girl who had helped capture the general, but I didn't want to lie to this man; besides, I was sure he wouldn't believe me. "What happened to the general?" I asked.

"He survived the war; he is back in Germany with a new family and a new life. He bears no grudge for his capture; he has visited me here in Delphi," said Manos Petrides. He paused and went on. "You asked what I believed about this strange story. I have sometimes thought that the stories the shepherds tell about the nymphs on the mountains are not imagination after all, that some of the old gods still live here at Delphi. Because I was watching when you came out of the rocks of Delphi. I had been watching a long time, and there was no one there. Then suddenly you were there. And who but one of the immortals would be completely unchanged after forty years, when I am now an old man with gray hairs?"

"It's not like that," I said. "I am really a quite ordinary American girl, though some strange things have happened to me. It's a fantastic story. I don't know if you'll believe it—"

"Miss Grant," said Manos Petrides, "I would say that I have no right to pry into your affairs except for one thing. Last night I told Nikos some of this. He was intrigued, but he said that there must be some ordinary explanation. This morning very early he went up to the ruins. An old school friend of his is now a guard and would let him in. This guard came to me a little while ago. While they were near the Temple, this guard looked away. When he looked back, Nikos was gone. They have searched all over the site; Nikos has vanished!"

# CHAPTER EIGHTEEN

For a moment the room seemed to blur, and I swayed on my feet. Manos put out his arms and held me gently. "No, I see that you are not a goddess," he said. "And perhaps I see something else as well." His eyes were compassionate, and his voice was soft. I shut my eyes and breathed deeply, trying to think.

"Nikos was carrying that headband that I tied his head up with next to his skin?" I asked. Manos Petrides nodded. "And he went up near the Temple, near the Rock of Sibyl?" He nodded again. I drew a deep breath. "Sit down, please, Kyrie Petrides," I said. "I'm going to tell you everything, and it may take a while."

When I had finished, Manos looked at me for a long time in silence, then smiled. "I believe you, Aleesah," he said quietly. "Because of what I have seen and because in that short time, I got to know you a little. But no one else at all would believe either of us. They would think that you are mad and that I am an old man who imagines crazy things about what happened long ago in the war. My wife sometimes teases me that I am still in love with that American girl I met so long ago."

At my startled glance he chuckled. "Perhaps a little then, my dear, but I am very happily married for many years. It is Nikos who loves you now, very much. Now perhaps I am just what the women now call male chauvinist, but I think that if you survived your adventures, Nikos will survive whatever adventure he is having. I am just an old farmer, but I read a great deal about things that interest me."

"Your English is much better now," I said with a smile. My

heart was suddenly lighter. Manos was right. Nikos was quite a man; if I had survived, why shouldn't he?

Manos chuckled. "Always since I have met you, I have had a good feeling for Americans. It caused me a little trouble with the Communists after the war, but it has helped me sometimes too. Yes, I have studied the English, and read about America, but also I study our history at Delphi. I think perhaps it is true that our ancestors were priests of Apollo, and that also may help Nikos. For now we will wait and hope. People here I will tell that I sent Nikos to Athens to get his head looked at. They will believe that; it is quite reasonable. Your journeys in time seemed to take very little of our time; perhaps Nikos will turn up any moment."

But that was days ago, days spent climbing around the slopes of Delphi in search of the Lines of Power, after repeated frustrating failures at the Rock. I've been writing my story down at odd moments to keep the details clear in my own mind and to see if I can find any clues that might suggest a way of finding my way into the Path again. I've tried to remember every word any of the Olympians ever said to me, and I reread the passages where I wrote them down, searching for any hints. Because the feeling is growing on me that Nikos will not return until I walk the Path once more. If he were going to return by himself, he would have done it by now.

Looking back to the beginning of what I have written, I see that I've caught up with the first things that I wrote down: my waking several mornings ago thinking I was late; my failure again at the Rock; my search for the Lines of Power. Every evening I spend at the Tholos, trying to contact Athena. I've even been back to Itea to swim, hoping to make contact there, but I have the feeling that the Path through the sea won't open again. I wonder if there's a clue in that.

The first time I went back and forth between the Rock of Sibyl and the Temple rock, and I suppose I've kept assuming that this is somehow the "normal" or "regular" way to reach the Path. But the second time I was in the Temple area, but not near the Rock; I came through darkness to a place away from the temple where

Dion's thiasos was gathered and returned via Amphissa. Then from the sea at Itea and back via the Rock of Sibyl; two returns via the Rock, but only one departure that way.

Should my last journey count as one or two? Call it two; I'd gone from the Tholos to the distant past and returned to the more recent past near the Rock. Then from the sea at Itea back to the sea near Itea again. Was there any kind of pattern here? The two times I hadn't returned via the Rock I'd returned to a person, Nikos Petrides. His last name has something to do with rocks; *petra* is the word for "rock." Anyway, certainly to me, Nikos is a rock to base hopes on.

But now I see that though I have *returned* via the Rock three times, I have started from it only once; every other time I have entered the Path somewhere else. Have I been looking in the wrong place for the entrance to the Path all these days? But I've tried the Tholos. I've tried the sea near Itea. I don't know where or how I entered the Path when I met Dionysos; trying to retrace that journey would be hopeless. But what else is there at Delphi that I haven't tried?

The answer comes to me as I write. The spring, the Castalian Spring! Surely there must be some kind of power there; it has always been intimately connected with the Delphic rites, always been the beginning, the entrance place for a journey to Delphi. It's too late today; I have an uneasy feeling about hunting for the Path in the dark, as if the literal darkness would somehow favor the Dark Powers. But tomorrow morning I'll go try my luck at the Castalian Spring. I'll leave this manuscript in my room, with a note to Kyria Amalia asking her to give it to Manos Petrides if I don't return. Because this time I feel that I will succeed. But what success will mean I'm almost afraid to think.

# EPILOGUE

My name is not Athena Pierce, and though I teach philosophy, it is not at Pacific Western University; there is no real university of that name, at least not in Washington State. Nor is my former student, who wrote this manuscript, really named Alice Grant. I've also changed other names and altered incidents a little so that real people won't be bothered by anyone who takes this story seriously. The man who is called Manos Petrides in this story brought me this manuscript a week after Alice disappeared without a trace. His son also has never reappeared. Manos believes this story implicitly and swears that the details about the abduction of General Kroenig are absolutely correct and include things that no one else alive knew.

Do I believe it? I don't know. I don't suppose Alice thought I would ever see what she wrote about me, and I don't agree with all her assessments; but the factual details are correct so far as her visit with me in Athens is concerned. At my request, Manos has done some checking in Delphi. Everything that can be verified there checks out.

There's no question of checking Alice's journeys to the distant past, as I told her in Athens. A lot of the details agree with the myths and poems that have come down to us, but that might be taken as evidence for her story. There's been no news of either Alice or Nikos in the time since his father gave me this manuscript, and there's no real reason for them to disappear, together or singly. There are occasional rockfalls in the gorge out of which the water of the Castalian Spring flows, but there were no known ones around the time that Alice disappeared. Nikos, of course, could have suffered delayed effects from his accident and collapsed or wandered off with amnesia, but that doesn't really explain why no trace of him has been found.

So the facts can't really be checked. As for the theories, I'd really rather not believe in an open past or future-future view of Time; it's a rather unsettling view of reality to think that the past could be changed and the present along with it. On the other hand, I've often wondered if there isn't more reality behind the stories of the Greek gods, the Olympians, than any modern scholar would allow. They seem so real, so individual in the stories that have come down to us, and the same personality seems to appear in stories from very different times and places.

So much for facts and theories. What follows is speculation. Grant for the sake of argument that everything in Alice Grant's story is true. What could have happened to Alice and Nikos? Reading over the manuscript, I've wondered whether Nikos—and perhaps Alice following after him—may have gone into the future this time rather than into the past. I'm sure that Delphi will be here as long as the planet lasts and will still be visited for its beauty and history.

But once Alice and Nikos had seen the future, I wonder whether whatever powers rule the Path would let them return. Tour buses and research projects would mean nothing to a Bronze Age Greek, but nowadays we're so future-oriented, so full of speculations about the future; I wonder if it wouldn't be dangerous for us to know too much about it.

Perhaps I'm quite wrong. I'm sure Alice was sincere, but perhaps her experiences were merely dreams or hallucinations and Manos is merely deceiving himself about her identity with the American girl he once knew briefly and could never forget. Maybe her story is true, and Alice and Nikos lived out their lives and died at some period in the past history of Delphi, perhaps as the Pythia and Priest of Apollo. The Pythias were supposed to be unmarried, of course, but one story that's told is that they began choosing the Pythias from among older women after a Pythia ran off with a young man. . . .

I'll be going back to America myself soon, back to my husband and daughters. I don't know what I'll tell Alice's family when I see them face-to-face; that depends a lot on my assessment of them. I'll tell my husband because we share everything, and I think that he'll believe Alice's story. But I'm still not sure whether I do myself.

Before I leave Delphi, I'll try to get up to the site early and look at the Rock of Sibyl, wondering what secrets it hides. I don't expect to see any mists rise from it or any trace of Alice or Nikos, but perhaps I'll come away with some kind of reassurance. Or perhaps not. I am sure that Alice and Nikos loved each other, and love is never wasted. I am sure that there is a struggle between Light and Darkness and that we should each do what we can to serve the true Light. And I believe and hope that a little of that true Light shines from Delphi, even in our dark and troubled times, shines for us all, but especially for Nikos and Alice.